The Midnight Diary of Zoya Blume

LAURA SHAINE CUNNINGHAM

The Midnight Diary of Zoya Blume

LAURA GERINGER BOOKS
An Imprint of HarperCollins*Publishers*

The Midnight Diary of Zoya Blume

Printed in the United States of America. For information address HarperCollins Children's Books, a division of HarperCollins Publishers, 1350 Avenue of the Americas, New York, NY 10019.
www.harperchildrens.com

Library of Congress Cataloging-in-Publication Data
Cunningham, Laura.
The midnight diary of Zoya Blume / by Laura Cunningham.—1st ed.
p. cm.
Summary: Left in the care of a magical stranger while her adoptive mother is away, twelve-year-old Zoya Blume confides her deepest secrets in her midnight diary.
ISBN 0-06-072259-2 — ISBN 0-06-072260-6 (lib. bdg.)
[1. Fear—Fiction. 2. Coming of age—Fiction. 3. Mothers and daughters—Fiction. 4. Intercountry adoption—Fiction. 5. Adoption—Fiction. 6. Russian Americans—Fiction. 7. Diaries—Fiction.] I. Title.
PZ7.C9168 Mi 2005 2004018499
[Fic]—dc22 CIP
AP

Typography by Alicia Mikles
1 2 3 4 5 6 7 8 9 10

First Edition

This book is dedicated
with all my heart
to my darling daughters,
Alexandra Rose
and
Jasmine Zoie Cunningham

Table of Contents

The Midnight Diary of Zoya Blume

CHAPTER ONE

The Stone Girl

May 23, night

It is the middle of the night. My mother has vanished. Leon is here in her place. I can hear him moving around in my mother's room. I do not even want to think about him, about how it will be with just him and me here in 2B. I will have to face him in the morning. Until then, the night is mine.

I have covered Nicky's cage but I hear him pacing, the scratch of his cockatiel claws on the sandpaper perch. He is tossing seeds, and every few minutes, he utters a shriek, as if he too is alarmed by our sudden change in circumstances.

I sit at my desk and open the new diary that my mother gave me as our parting gift. I use the tiny key and pick up the purple-feathered pen. I begin to write in purple ink: "PRIVATE. The penalty for unlocking this diary without permission is Certain Death." I draw a skull and crossbones so anyone who breaks into this journal can see I am not kidding. Here I tell the truth about things.

I hear Leon outside my door.

"Are you all right?" he whispers through the door. "Are you hungry? Are you thirsty?"

"I'm fine," I lie.

"I saw your light," he says.

"I sleep with the light on," I call back, another lie.

I wonder if he knows I am lying. I overheard my mother's whispered instructions before she went away—what I eat, when I wake, how I take my keys to school, when I come home, how late I stay up . . . when I do my homework. She has told him I might have some "unusual requests"—especially in the middle of the night. "Do you know about night terrors?" I heard my mother whisper to Leon. "Zoya had nightmares as a little child. . . ." I did not hear the rest . . . her voice trailed off. The last thing I heard her say was "I left fresh-squeezed orange juice."

"See you in the morning," he says, his voice soft.

The truth is I don't want to see Leon in the morning; I want him to vanish and my mother to reappear. I want time to go backward, and everything to be the way it was before she left.

My mother says: "Your first memory is your point of view." But I must go far back in time, through a fog, to find my past. I think of my first memory as locked up in the little plaid suitcase I carried from the orphanage when I was four. I remember the suitcase, but I cannot, in my mind, open it and see what is inside. I know my mother saved that suitcase, but I have not seen it for a long time.

I have moved my favorite photograph of my mother to my desk. Mimi. She seems to smile at me, an encouraging smile. My mother is known for her smile. She has perfect white teeth. When she smiles, her eyes crinkle; when she laughs, her eyes have a secret sparkle. She loves to laugh.

Mimi is very pretty. She doesn't think she is pretty, but she is. Her red hair has a lot of energy; it curls and swings. You cannot miss my mother. She wears bright colors ("Hey," she says, laughing, "I'm not afraid to clash!") and she loves high heels and party dresses with rhinestones and diamonds. She has a great collection of party purses with jeweled clasps. And she lets me use her lipstick and eyeliner.

Mimi helped me paint my room violet, hot pink, and green. This room is decorated exactly the way I want it to look. I think it is just right, but other people have said, "I can't believe your mother let you have those colors." She even let me buy purple frames for my eyeglasses.

My mother makes her living by designing places like store windows and setups for pictures in magazines. She is a stylist. "If I can't make it better," Mimi always says, "I can at least make it beautiful." Her favorite color combinations are hot fuchsia, lavender, and yellow. She has the opposite taste from Gramma, who likes only black.

When we moved into 2B, we didn't dare throw away Gramma's furniture, but we disguised it in what I like to think of as the Girlie Renovation—we painted, papered, slip-covered, and draped every dark shape with a flowery print or bright color. This transformed Gramma's home into a brighter place by day or lamplight, but we could not hide everything. The clawed fangs and feet of Gramma's furnishings poke out from below our ruffled bed skirts and slipcovers, especially at night.

When I was smaller and we visited Gramma here, I would sit on the floor. I used to hide under my mother's skirt as if it were a tent. I held on to her stockinged legs, because I was sure the chairs would pounce on me. I could see through the filtered cloth of her skirt and hear Gramma's disapproval: "She is clingy, Mimi, that child is too clingy. You have to break her of these bad habits."

"She's scared of your chair," my mother would say. And that was the truth—Gramma sat in her monster chair; it had winged arms and huge nails on its clawed feet. The feet clutched big balls, and the armrests ended in dragon faces, with bared wooden teeth.

I was so scared, I seldom looked past Gramma's black laced shoes and her peach-colored, knotted stockings. Her legs had a sad, heavy look, as if they weighed too much to move very well. She stamped her feet fiercely sometimes, when she wanted her dinner or her coffee. And she used a stick—not a curved cane, but a walking stick, with a snarling face on the knob. Everywhere I looked in Gramma's apartment there was some creature making a face at me.

In fact, when Gramma lived here, I was scared of this entire building. It seemed like a castle with its high arched entrance, walled courtyard, diamond-paned windows, and mysterious corridors. Everything my mother admired about Gramma's building—the giant lobby and "spacious" apartments—made me feel small and frightened.

Gramma's building is called Roxy's Mansion—it is a gray stone apartment house with a turret. Big crouching granite lions guard the entry steps on either side of the front door. The only thing I liked here in those days was the Stone Girl with her waving marble hair. I wondered if she was a statue or a real girl turned to stone in a spell. Was she Roxy?

I still love the Stone Girl. She is so graceful—she always seems about to dance. One stone hand is outstretched, and her small marble foot is raised. Her carved tunic seems to flutter. She is almost naked underneath—her small breasts are not showing, but I can see an outline.

If she could see, the Stone Girl could look into my room, but her eyes, though carved to appear open, are blind. She smiles a soft, ancient smile of recognition. "Do I know you?" she seems to ask. At some point in the distant past, a fountain was inserted on the top of her head, and the water from the spout streaked rivulets of rust, like bleeding tears down her stone cheeks.

Sometimes, when no one is watching, I climb onto the fountain, my fingers digging into the cracked marble. I have climbed high enough on the statue to look into her unseeing eyes. At those times, I feel that she has a secret. And her smile is a promise.

My mother grew up here in 2B. I can understand why she refused to move back into the building until Gramma moved out last spring. Gramma was always saying gloomy things to her like "Go out. Leave me alone. Alone as a stone." My mother had been sad, growing up in this apartment. Is it my turn now? Does this building hold a shadow curse of unhappiness and fear?

The first night in Roxy's Mansion, my mother lit sparklers in the courtyard and we pretended to dance with the Stone Girl. My mother said we were celebrating our new start in life. Now my mother is gone and I have only her special bathrobe, the pink chenille robe with the carved cabbage roses, to comfort me. Before my mother tiptoed outside, she placed her robe on top of me and whispered good-bye. Actually, she did not say, "Good-bye," she said, "Later, later, Sweetheart."

I pretended to be asleep, but the minute she left, I jumped up and went to my window to watch my mother go. She was walking fast across the courtyard, white with moonlight, to a waiting yellow taxicab. My mother hurried past the Stone Girl and then disappeared, like someone walking out of a frame in a film. I was left staring at the Stone Girl. For an instant, it seemed to me that the statue, so thinly dressed in her stone-carved veil, shivered. But of course, the Stone Girl cannot move.

The truth is, we have not lived long enough in this apartment to trust it. The instant my mother walked out, my room darkened and shadows filled the corners. Quickly I had to turn on all my lights, even the bathroom light, and pull the light cord in my closet. Light will keep away the creature of darkness, that thing I call the Buka.

I never talk about the Buka. I know I am taking a chance even acknowledging her here, in my diary. The nature of monsters is that they thrive on belief. They can gain strength every time you mention them. My mother says, "If you don't believe in the Buka, she will disappear."

I don't know for sure if the Buka is alive or a ghost. I saw her only once—out of the corner of my eye—a long time ago. She is not human, or animal, but is composed of darkness; she falls upon you as a shadow, and then you disappear. She can appear as one huge dark creature, or she can shred into a cloud of several winged black shapes that reunite as they close over your head.

I try so hard not to think about the Buka, but she almost caught me once. I remember being smothered in the black gauze of her folds, but I cannot remember the rest. The Buka knows she had me long ago; she knows I fear her—and that gives her the power to return. I cannot control my fear, even though I know it feeds her and allows her to swell. She has often hidden at the top of my closet, in a black corner. All winter, I refused to reach up there for my sweaters, because I knew she was waiting.

The Buka can assume any shape, fill any room. She can grow as tall as the closet and fill out its sides. She can squeeze under my bed and flatten herself there, compressed between the box spring and the floor. The Buka likes dark hallways and unlit bathrooms. One time she almost got me: She was hiding behind the shower curtain, but I caught her movement and flipped the light switch, and she had to disappear. I never tell anyone when the Buka tries to catch me; I just keep quiet and turn on more lights.

My floor lamp, next to the desk, has three strengths—bright, brighter, and brightest. Now that my mother has left, I tug the cord and raise my light to the highest power. The globe glows warm peach under a fringed violet shade.

Outside my window, the world has turned moon white. The courtyard trees are in bud, but as I watched my mother go, a chill wind blew and the blossoms fell like an out-of-season snow.

"Seven days," my mother promised. "You know I always keep my word to you. Seven days and I'll come home. Count them in your diary; on the seventh day I'll be home. Have I ever lied to you?"

I turn to the page of my diary marked May 30—my birthday. I write: "My mother is home!" And yet I don't believe my mother will keep her promise this time. Why do I doubt her, when she has always told me the truth?

When I cried, "Don't go!" I thought my mother would change her mind. She gave me her reason—but no matter how often she explained why she had to leave, and why it was so sudden, I could not really believe her. Her voice went high, the way mine does when I lie.

Gramma always uses this one word about my mother that I hate—*permissive*. Gramma says it with the pruney look on her mouth she has when she drinks cough syrup or takes one of the many pills she keeps in her round medicine compact.

"Mimi is too permissive, too permissive; she will regret it one day."

"Don't pay attention to what Gramma says—she doesn't know what she is saying; she is seventy-eight, and the blood doesn't reach her brain anymore," my mother whispers.

So I picture Gramma with her blood just

going up to her neck or her nose, and no blood to the brain, so the brain is a sponge that has dried out, and only the sticky poisons remain. I imagine the poisons stick in her throat too, giving her voice that croaking sound.

There is a *knock knock*. Leon. He is back. Is he spying on me?

"Are you okay?" he says.

For a moment, I want to scream, "Go away. I am *not* okay. I want my mother, *not* you!"

I feel the heat of anger rush to my face, and I can recall the force of past rages, the thunder of my own stamping feet, my clenched fists.

"I'm fine," I say again to the man on the other side of the door, where my mother should be. "Everything is fine!"

I write in the diary: "Everything is weird. I want Leon to disappear." I don't even remember him, just that he sent presents to me when I was small. When I hear the name Leon, I think of a gift box, and a card with his name on it—"Leon sent this for your birthday"; "Leon sent this for Christmas"; "Leon sent this from Europe . . ."

"There's no one else to move in here with you for a whole week," my mother said. "And I have to leave right away. Leon is happy to come; he's looking forward to it." She smiled. "Believe me, Leon is the best person. We're lucky he is free. The only other choice is Gramma."

"Anyone but Gramma!" I said.

I listen to Leon walk back into my mother's room. I hear him go into my mother's bathroom, and the sound of the shower running full blast.

This is my chance, I think. I must run out while he is in the shower. I want to get to the hall closet and look for my plaid suitcase. If I find it now, maybe I will remember more, from that gray time in Russia, that frozen time before my mother carried me home.

"Someday," my mother promised, "you will know all the secrets."

"Why not now?" I wanted to know.

"You're not ready."

"Well, how do I get ready?"

"You go through life, you have . . . experiences."

Before she left, she handed me my diary,

with the key. "I want you to keep a record, but it's your secret. You don't have to show it to me." She demonstrated how to lock and unlock the diary. "Now hide the key," she said.

I open my bedroom door to the hall just a crack—is Leon really in the shower? Or is he running the water and standing outside? I know I have to hurry—I have only a minute to get to the closet, search for my suitcase, and bring it back to my room. I drag along my chair so I can reach high.

The hall looks empty, except for Gramma's china cabinet, which is occupied by dozens of tiny china figurines. Inside the cabinet, there are porcelain girls in aproned skirts and bonnets and boys in caps and buttoned trousers. They curtsy to one another, holding fishing poles. There are dozens of them, a happy family. And the china people have little china pets—kittens that reach up with fixed paws, puppies that pose on their hind legs, even a lamb with a blue bow tied around its neck.

"Don't touch them!" Gramma always said whenever I reached for the glass. This cabinet is always locked. Gramma hid the key. I wanted to handle the little china children and their pets, work them into my stories the way I did with my doll, Natalie, but Gramma said, "No, you will break them and they cost a fortune. This is my collection. They are very valuable." Everything Gramma owns is "valuable."

On my last birthday, she gave me a set of smaller china children. They were cheerful too, with the same rosy porcelain cheeks, and they dipped and curtsied in permanent poses. My favorite is the milkmaid, who holds two buckets. The buckets are done in great detail—there are even droplets of milk in a frozen splash.

Gramma said, "I am giving you these little figures, but I want you to keep them safe in the glass case. They are not toys. They are valuables. They are not to play with—they are to save."

I had felt my blood rise. What? I could not even play with them? I would be so careful; I would not break them. What good would they be if I could not touch them?

My mother gave me a look that said: "You can play with them later, just don't tell Gramma."

That is what is nice about my mother; she understands that some rules need to be broken. Whenever I get sick, my mother lets me take all the figurines out of the case and play with them on my bed.

Now, in the light reflected through my open door, the china figurines glisten. They almost look alive, as if I surprised them at some midnight play. As I pass, the figurines tremble. The cabinet is unsteady, standing on its own thin-clawed feet. I move slowly, so as not to rattle it.

I see the big gold candy box locked inside the cabinet too—Gramma's special imported chocolates. When I used to visit Gramma here, she always said at the end of our time together, "You can have a candy now," and she opened the golden tin and pulled out a wrapped chocolate. I made that chocolate last, melting it on my tongue, not speaking until it had dissolved. She watched me eat it, and that spoiled my pleasure a little bit, but not so completely as to ruin it entirely. Her watching me eat the chocolate was part of the gift, I guess.

For a minute, I think of how good the candy tastes, and how maybe I could unlock the cabinet and have a chocolate. But there is no time; it is more important to get my plaid suitcase.

It is hard to move quietly—I feel like an elephant dragging my desk chair so that I can reach the top shelf of the closet. The chair legs knock against the wall.

I hear the shower stop running in my mother's room. I imagine Leon toweling off, drying himself with my mother's big thick bath towels.

I open the closet door and position my chair. I stop—two beady eyes flash at me from within the closet! I almost scream but catch myself in time—a fox is glaring at me from the closet rack! Will it pounce and sink its fangs into my neck?

Then I remember—the fox is not alive. The closet is filled with Gramma's out-of-season furs . . . all with beady eyes and pointy teeth. Gramma lives in Florida now, where she doesn't need fur, so the fox waits here, black eyes glinting, white fangs bared. . . . He waits for Gramma to return, for snow, and winter. . . .

I wedge into the closet and climb onto the chair. I am so nervous, the chair shakes and I almost tip over. Frantically I pull the light cord. There are two shelves at the top of the closet. On the first shelf is a see-through plastic box holding stacks of ribboned letters. I can guess they are love letters. But who wrote them?

On the highest shelf, I think I see my old plaid suitcase, lying sidewise. I try to reach up, but even standing on the chair I can't get to it. So I grab the plastic box stuffed with letters belonging to my mother. I hear Leon, he is moving toward the hall door. I clutch the box and jump down. It's all I can do to drag the chair and run. My mother's bathrobe is almost falling off and I nearly trip, crashing into Gramma's china cabinet on my way to my room. I hear the sickening tinkle of china figurines toppling and breaking. I do not stop to see who is broken.

"Zoya!" Leon is shouting now. "What happened? What's wrong?"

I don't answer but run as fast as I can and slam the door, fearful he will open it and catch me, punish me.

"Zoya!" he is shouting as he runs toward my door. "Zoya! What has happened? What's wrong? Did something break?"

CHAPTER TWO

The Secret of Life

May 24, midnight!

My heart hammers. Quick! Leon will be in my room in a minute! I stash the letter box under my bed beneath the ruffled skirt. *Just in time!* I can hear Leon right outside my door.

My cockatiel, Nicky, is screeching under his cover. I love Nicky, but his shrieking is not helpful in an emergency like this. "Sshh!" I warn him, and peek under the birdcage cover so he can see it is only me. Nicky looks back—he is maybe the prettiest cockatiel in the world. My mother gave him to me, and I love him so much. He has apricot blush circles like rouge on his cheeks, and a high golden crown, which right now is poking straight up because he is as scared as I am! I can tell that Nicky, like me, longs for a normal night when he might perch on my shoulder while I watch TV. He loves comedies, and squawks when the TV characters laugh, and clucks at the sad parts. "Sshh!" I whisper. "Don't give me away!" Nicky looks at me, cocking his head.

I jump into bed and pull the comforter up, almost over my head. I shut my eyes; Leon is opening my door. This is the moment I dread—Leon enters my room.

My mother says Leon is not a stranger; he is her best friend from long ago. But he is a stranger to me. I remind myself that Leon gave me many of my best Christmas and birthday presents—exotic things from far away, like the real grass hula skirt, the silk sari, the giant stuffed giraffe, the ballet tutu, and the cowgirl suit complete with holsters. But I still can't quite picture him.

Now he is standing over me, and by just peeking through my squinted lids, I can make out a tall, dark, skinny form. He is barefoot, wearing a pajama top and jeans. "What happened?" he is asking.

"Nothing," I murmur.

"I heard a crash. Something fell. Something broke."

"Not in here," I squeak. "I think the china cabinet . . . it shakes sometimes. Go see."

Leon turns and investigates the cabinet right outside my door.

"Oh, boy," he says. "I didn't see this coming. I wonder if these were valuable."

I am wondering too—who is broken? Is it the little china boy, or my curtsying girl? Not the milkmaid, I pray.

"Do you want this lamp out?" Leon is asking. His hand moves under the tasseled shade.

"No," I say, squeezing my eyes shut and making my voice all muffly, like I am half asleep. "I like to sleep with a light on!"

"I could read to you, or we could just sit and talk?" he offers. His voice is deep and soft.

My mother says, "Never whine," but I kind of whine so he thinks I am not really awake.

He waits, and I wonder: Is the letter box poking out from under my bed? I think I hid it well enough, but maybe something is showing.

Finally Leon sighs and exits. I look at my room—there are big wet footprints on my violet rug where he has walked. I jump out of bed and kneel. To my relief, the box is still there, well hidden. But when I try to lift the lid, it will not open. I try with my nail file, but it is seriously locked.

Under my bed, I spot my favorite shoes, the red sparkly ruby slippers. I know they are an important piece of the puzzle. My mother gave them to me years ago and said they were special because the shoes have to do with her own first memory, her own point of view.

I wiggle my feet into the ruby slippers, conjuring Dorothy from *The Wizard of Oz*. She clicked her heels and her home was restored. If I click them, will my mother return?

"Write it all down," my mother said. "Write the truth in the diary. It will help you, Zoya, through each day and night."

The clock on the church down the street

chimes midnight. The wooden cuckoo clock in my bedroom agrees. Twelve chimes. Nicky, under his cover, squawks. I hear, as if in answer, the coo of pigeons, so loud they seem very near. *Coo, coo*, they cry; maybe they are on my windowsill, feeling cold and lost too.

Wearing the red shoes, I go back to my desk and I take up the purple pen . . . but nothing happens. Then I shut my eyes tight and will myself back to the beginning, so many years ago. First memory, come!

I cannot see it, but I can taste it—something tastes sweet and sour—not food, but cloth; I am sucking on the satin edge of a blanket. The blanket, once peach, is faded to a pale pearl gray. My Mickey. I am hungry. And my fingers are working too, in a rhythm, working my special blanket, fraying its satin edges.

It is summer; I remember the feel of cool bed linen. I throw back my arms against the pillowcases, and then trail my fingers, chilling my fingernails against the cloth. Suddenly, summer fades and my body is curled, for warmth, knees to my belly. At my back, the wind whistles under the windowpane, and creeps under my covers. *Russia*. Even the name—*Russia*—comes in as an ice blast, *Russia*. I hear the *sssssh*, the hush of falling snow, the whisper of sleet, needling. *Sssssh,* the Russian wind hisses. *Keep the secrets*.

I come from a country that I cannot remember and whose name even now makes me shiver. Is this a memory or a bad dream? Do I remember Russia? I remember flashes; I remember bits like hot tea in a glass. A different kind of chocolate, dark, almost black, not so sweet.

I am alone, alone in my bed; or is it a cage? I see bars. A crib. The crib cage is painted green, a dark green, and the paint flakes, like dried leaves. I am alone as a stone in this crib, but not alone in the room. I am aware of someone else, someone breathing, someone moaning. . . .

I am so cold. My feet are freezing. I hear the sound of boots scraping, and an icicle chandelier hangs outside my window. The world outside is glass. I hold a milk bottle, and the milk flows slowly, thickened with ice crystals, like slush.

Someone is telling a bedtime story about an old couple who have no children of their own, so they build one out of snow. . . . The little white snow maiden is so perfect that the old childless couple wish her into coming alive. The little snow girl does come alive, and dances and plays. She is so delightful, they treat her as a daughter, and everyone loves one another, but then something goes terribly wrong. . . .

Now my brain curls up like a hamster in my skull; I do not want to know more. I shrink from the memory, and, in turn, the memory shrinks and almost disappears. I will the memory to return. Now there is a smell—the smell of cleaning liquid, sharp in my nose. I can feel a pain in my stomach. I have to go to the bathroom, but I do not dare let go. If I do, the wet will turn the sheets colder and I will freeze.

Is this my first memory—the numb struggle to avoid freezing in the gray light of dawn? I try to see—who else is in that room? How did I get there? *Where is my mother?* Through an effort of willpower, I stiffen into a statue of myself. Am I the Stone Girl? Is this my point of view?

I can feel a draft of fear, the creep of a shadow coming between my first memory and me. But my mother's memory, light and sparkling, returns—

"The first thing *I* can remember," my mother told me, "is Gramma spanking me and taking away my Dorothy *Wizard of Oz* shoes—I wanted to wear them to school!"

"So what is your point of view?" I wanted to know.

"My point of view," my mother said, taking a package out of the closet, "is that I want it sparkly—I want it sparkly every day. Gramma threw away my shoes." She grinned. "But I found them again in the garbage. I saved them all these years—for you."

That was when she gave me the ruby slippers and I asked, "May I wear them to school?"

"I insist!" she said.

They still fit me perfectly. My feet are small. I am too small for twelve in every way. Stunted is Gramma's diagnosis. It was "poor nutrition," my mother says. "You're just petite, not a big galumphing girl like I was! I always had to bend my knees to dance with the boys."

It is strange how, if you write, the writing takes over. It is as if my purple-feathered pen can write my story all on its own. The pen does not want to stop; the pen remembers what I have forgotten.

Another memory: Mimi is carrying me.

"Four is too old to carry. Make her walk." Gramma's voice screeches, like my bird Nicky's but not so friendly. Nicky squawks when he is excited; Gramma shrieks because she is always angry. Gramma says, "She's so small and sickly, and who knows what else is wrong with her? She's damaged. It is not normal how she cries so much at night." In my memory, I don't see Gramma's face. I only hear her, and see her feet and ankles, thick, in heavy black shoes.

The memory makes my eyes hurt, and my forehead feel hot. I start to burn, and I suspect I am getting one of my fevers. I get sick a lot. I have what my mother calls "low resistance." I imagine my tonsils as inflamed red balls with white polka dots. There was talk of removing them because they were "bad." Should I take some cough drops? My mother always stocks them in my medicine cabinet. *Uh-oh. No, I can't get sick, here alone with Leon.* But maybe if I was sick enough, he would call my mother and she would rush home.

I go to the medicine cabinet and pull out the thermometer. It is one of those ear gadgets. I feel like I am shooting myself in the head. I hold the pistol-shaped plastic thermometer pointed into my ear and count to a hundred. My temperature, I see, is normal. Actually, it is maybe a little below normal. Maybe the drafts of memory have chilled me from the inside out.

I reach for my cough drops and open the box. A note falls out, and I recognize my mother's delicate handwriting, slanted to the left—"If you find this, your throat hurts. Take two, and drink lots of juice. I know you get scared when you feel sick, but don't worry—you will get well quickly! Remember 'the secret.' Write it down in the diary, just the way you told it to me!"

I know what she is referring to—the last time I got sick, I had a mysterious experience, almost as mysterious as Dorothy riding a tornado to Oz. It would be embarrassing to tell anyone. The single soul who knows is my mother, because she was in the other room when it happened to me. . . .

I was lying on the sofa, and she was squeezing oranges for fresh juice in the kitchen. Hot waves of fever swept through me. I began to feel myself drift between the living-room couch and the movie on the screen, into a whole other realm . . . I could not tell where one began and the other ended. I soared to a higher place. I tell no one this, but I can tell it here. I flew! Not really, I guess, but I could sense the ache of wings spreading from between my shoulder blades. I sailed aloft, billowing upward, caught by faraway winds.

Do I dare write this? My mother says: "Write it down, write it all down." *That day, I learned the Secret of Life and the secret cured me.*

I squeeze my eyes shut, open them, and see what I saw then—the golden dots, every dot elongating to become a dash, and the dashes connecting to form a message spelled out in the sunshine of our living room, caught in iridescence right here in 2B. I reached up, as if I could touch it. And for a minisecond, I grasped the truth, the ultimate truth—the secret. Then the light became a column that swirled and rose, like a dancer, just past my reach. I stood and tried to dance among the columns of light. But as soon as I passed into the light, it vanished. My hands grasped at the air . . . at the swirling ultralucent forms I knew were there.

I called my mother and she came running. I told her: "I just saw the secret . . . dancing lights . . . but now it's gone."

"That happens," she said.

"You've seen them too?" I asked.

My mother gave me a smile as radiant as those magical lights. "Oh, yes, I saw lights, the night I first saw you. I knew they were a sign; that I was not alone in the world anymore now that I had a beautiful daughter!"

As I write this down, I can almost see those lights again; they spin and glow.

"Will I see the secret lights again?"

"I think so," my mother said, "but maybe they will only return when—" She broke off, and I suddenly knew what she was thinking. I could almost hear her think, like a ticking clock. I had exchanged the Secret of Life for the even stranger secret of being able to hear my mother think. And she was thinking: *"when we die."*

I grab my Mickey, wrapping it around me, over my mother's robe. I am shivering now. Is it a fever? My throat feels sore, even though I am sucking the lemon cough drops. I sit bundled up at the desk, and I reach for my doll, Natalie.

I cannot remember a time when I did not have Natalie. I have held her so long, her scarlet silk skirt has frayed and is falling to shreds. I have kissed her painted face so many times that her lips are no longer red. Her eyes do not move—they are painted also—which gives Natalie a fixed stare. She looks wide-eyed and startled, as if she saw something she did not expect. I hold and comfort her.

Natalie has a hollow center and no legs underneath her skirt. She has no real breasts either, just a molded shape without detail. I lift her skirt above her head and study her white porcelain body. She is like a cone. Sometimes I hide things inside Natalie's hollow cone body, beneath her skirt where no one will find them. I trust her to keep my secrets. I hide the key to this diary here. Natalie will guard it.

My mother says I was holding Natalie when we left the hospital in Russia and someone tried to take her back, but I refused to let go. My mother said, "Let her keep the doll," and gave them money in exchange. Natalie's secret is she can't sleep without me. Her eyes never shut. Only I can tell when she feels safe enough to sleep—her eyes glaze over and go blank.

Tonight Natalie gives me her most reassuring look. But the light outside my window has whitened, tinged with the violet blues of midnight. Inside 2B, shadows have gathered and I can feel stirrings in Gramma's furniture, which threatens to come alive—the face in the headboard of my canopied bed grins, not in a nice way, like the Buka trapped in wood.

The one time the Buka almost seized me, I flipped on the bathroom light switch, but the light only flashed, signaling her. The room went black and the Buka filled it, her soft amorphous sides reaching every tiled wall. My mother came running in and said, "Oh, the light is out." But I knew.

"Blew a fuse, that's all." I could not get over my mother's courage, staying in the dark bathroom. Then the light flared and banished the Buka—I saw her shadow scoot from the bathroom.

I suspect the Buka has now seeped into the heat vent, a small mesh-covered square door inset near my window. A pouf of dust is coming from this opening. I am almost certain this is where the Buka is hiding, peeking out at my room, waiting for an opportunity. I push the wastebasket in front of the vent so she cannot spy on me.

The Buka cannot appear when there is too much light. I turn on my extra night-light—the pink electric candle tip—to continually flare through every night, right above the vent, so there can be no quick entrances and exits. Now that the vent is blocked, I wonder: Can the Buka use the dumbwaiter or the incinerator shafts to get down to the basement?

The basement is the best hideout of all, a vast network of shadowed corridors and dark cobwebbed rooms. Down there, the Buka can breed, divide, and reassemble, sneaking into grates and up to the other apartments.

In my mother's absence the barriers are broken. I am frightened. Nicky, under his cage cover, feels it too. He continues to shriek, and from somewhere eerily close by comes an answering coo.

If only I can keep the diary day-by-day, night-by-night, perhaps I can keep the Buka away. I flip the dated pages ahead again to May 30, when my mother has promised to return. Shakily I add to what I've already written: "Happy ending." I just have to get there. May 30. All I have to do is survive seven days.

Everyone in Roxy's Mansion is asleep except me. And Leon. I can hear him walking around in the living room. I can tell he is trying not to make a sound, but I concentrate and I can hear his very soft footfalls. The harder he tries to be silent, the better I can hear him. I hear the vacuum snap of the refrigerator door. Did he just drink juice from the bottle? That's not allowed.

Then I hear him go to my mother's room, and the door clicks. Silence. The more I listen, the more I can hear—a chirp in my smoke detector, battery low. I hear an answer from under the cage cover—Nicky, talking to the smoke detector. His chirp is sleepy now. I hear what must be the pigeons again—*coo, coo, coo*.

Then I hear a new sound, faint and coming from far away, from down below. It is a thin wail. A cry. Not words, just cries . . . weak and helpless sounding.

Who could be crying? I concentrate again—the sound is downstairs. I check the courtyard again. The Stone Girl is even more ghostly now—something white has settled like a cape across her shoulders and is thickening around her bare stone feet. Her head is veiled in the lace of falling blossoms.

And then I hear the cry again—more pleading than before. Is the Stone Girl crying? I tiptoe to my door, turn the knob. Outside my room, the hall is narrow. The door to my mother's room is shut, but sounds are coming from within—music, soft and distant, a sad song, with the strum of a lone guitar. And the cooing—how is it possible? The pigeon coo seems to come from within my mother's room! It is distinct, louder, as I approach the door.

Coo. Coo. Coo.

Now Leon is singing along with the radio. He sings, "'Yesterday . . . Why she had to go, I don't know . . . Oh I believe in yesterday.'"

I run, not back to my room, but to the heavy door that seals 2B from the rest of the building. I move the dead-bolt pole, shifting the lock, and open the door. Out in the hall, the crying is even more distinct.

On laundry trips down to the basement with my mother, I have seen nothing to invite my return alone. The cellar is a gray netherworld of belching furnace, incinerator, and chain-link-fenced off-limits areas. A hunk of native rock, a small mountain of granite, is incorporated into one small section, but for the most part, the basement is a long gray hall with chambers and subchambers, most of them unlit. Each room seems to lead to a deeper darkness beyond, like a cavern, or a dungeon.

Mr. Uzzle, the super, lives down there, with Spike, his pit bull. Spike has a nude pink face, black eye patches, and bared teeth. He strains, behind a barred gate, toward anyone who approaches the sanctuary of The Super. There is a sign that says DANGER. BEWARE OF DOG. Spike is Mr. Uzzle's Cerberus, and his basement is Hades, home base of the Buka.

The basement vents breathe forth plumes of gray dust, and buzzing sounds—the hum and groan of the machinery of Roxy's Mansion. One can hear the crackle of flame from within the incinerator where garbage burns. There is also the scuttling noise of falling trash, as more garbage falls down the chute. I have thoughts of falling down the chute and going up in smoke. But now I feel an irresistible urge to descend the service stairway that blares a red warning with an exclamation point: DO NOT ENTER EMERGENCY EXIT ONLY! to investigate the cries down below.

The minute I exit, the heavy door of 2B

swings backward, snapping shut. *Click*. The door has locked behind me. I stand, paralyzed, on the straw welcome mat. I look down at my ruby slippers; I am standing in my nightgown, with my mother's long bathrobe trailing. I am alone in the hallway, locked out.

The hallway light winces on and off, a fluorescent ring near the exit stair. The ring seems fueled by a fading power source. If the light fails completely, I will be plunged into darkness. And then the Buka will have me—black cloak spreading wide and blending with the night.

CHAPTER THREE

Leon

May 24, 1 A.M.

The peephole suddenly flickers and I can see the lens dilate, like a human eye. Leon sees me.

"It's me, Zoya!" I cry. "Please let me in!"

I start to cry. If I don't get back inside, I will die. The light flickers, and in the darker intervals, I sense the Buka near, coming nearer, waiting for a total eclipse of light.

The faint cries from far below rise also, a chorus of complaint, but all I want now is to get back inside 2B, where it is warm and well-lit, and run to my room, to Natalie, to my bed, and hide until this strange night has passed.

The door swings inward, and there he is—Leon, in a black satin cape and top hat, with two white doves on his shoulders.

We both gasp and cry out the identical greeting—"*Is that you?*"

He is almost seven feet tall, taller with the top hat, and although his eyes are a twinkle-blue and he is smiling, my first impression is of Dracula, on the doorstep of 2B.

Before I scream, I realize: *Oh, the doves were the ones cooing in my mother's room*.

"What are you doing out there?" he says.

"I'm locked out," I gasp. "*What are you doing?*"

I see he is holding a black wand with a white tip.

"Rehearsing," he answers. "Come back inside."

Something in his smile, despite a chipped white front tooth, reassures me.

At least he doesn't yell, like the super, Mr. Uzzle. Leon says, "I'm surprised you would leave the apartment in the middle of the night. When I looked in on you, you seemed to be asleep."

"I heard sounds in the basement," I tell him. "I was going to investigate."

"I think basement sounds are better investigated in the morning." He leads me back to my mother's room, and through the open door I can see he has hung up a banner, black silk with gold-and-purple embroidered writing: THE ASTOUNDING ARMAND AND SONAMBULA.

"I thought your name was Leon," I say.

"My stage name is The Astounding Armand," Leon says. "I'm a magician."

"Will you make me disappear?" I ask. As soon as I say this, I wonder if somehow he made my mother disappear.

"Only if you want to disappear," he says, smiling. "I like to disappear myself; I have no known address."

"But you must live somewhere?"

He waves his wand at a large, black, shining trunk. "I live out of my trunk. I stay in hotels, mostly. Sometimes I take such long trips, I sleep on trains or in cabins on a ship. I travel almost all the time."

I can't help but be curious about his trunk—

the lid is open, and profusions of colored silks, diamond wands, and veils are visible.

"Can I see?" I ask. He hesitates, and I wait for him to make some reference to the fact that it is the middle of the night, but he does not seem to care.

"I can show you some things," he says, "but not everything. When you become a licensed magician, you have to take an oath never to give away a trick, except to another licensed magician. I took that oath when I was seventeen and I have lived by it. I might be able to tell you a few things, but not the tricks protected by the Society of Magicians."

A shimmering gold cape and costume catch my eye. It has diamonds and rubies sewn on it, and I see a big matching tiara, and long, gold silk gloves.

"Whose costume is that?" I want to know.

"Well, I used to work with an assistant. Sonambula." Leon's face changes, and I can't tell if the memory makes him happy or sad. By the soft way he says her name, I know he loves this girl, Sonambula.

Did Sonambula die? I wonder. "Will she ever return?" I ask.

"No" is his answer. He snaps shut the big theatrical trunk.

"I can show you the bird act," he offers. "It isn't covered under the sacred oath." Then he adds, "The birds took a pledge of their own: the Bird Oath."

"Did they coo?"

"You bet," Leon says, keeping a straight face. "These birds are brother and sister, and they are the best in the business."

Leon shows me how he has set up a home for his doves in my mother's bedroom. The doves don't live in cages, like Nicky. They occupy boxes, with veils draped across the tops. When the white doves coo, they sound just like pigeons.

"Meet Laverne," he introduces, "and MacDougall."

With one grand gesture, he whisks the doves onto his wand and proffers the wand to me, like a perch. The birds are snowy white with rounded chests and bright-red eyes. They coo in unison.

"They're not pets," Leon says. "They're working birds, part of the act. They're members of the Magician Bird Union, but we can see if they'll perform a little for you."

"What do they do?" I ask. I never saw a pigeon do anything magical.

"Watch this."

Leon takes one dove, the fatter one, Laverne, and turns her upside down in his palm. "You can hold her," he suggests. "Just don't turn her right side up—that will break the spell."

I hold Laverne. She lies still, warm and soft, upside down in my hand, her small yellow scaled feet curled upon her chest. Her electric-red eyes shut. She does appear under a spell. "Is she all right?" I ask.

"She's hypnotized," Leon explains. "This is how you hypnotize a dove." He turns MacDougall on his hand, and the bird assumes the same Sleeping Beauty pose.

"You're a hypnotist?"

"Not exactly," he answers. "Come see. . . ."

I follow him, the sleeping bird in my hand. I still don't know if I should trust Leon. His lopsided grin and bright eyes, the color of sapphires, are not at all scary, but his cloak is too reminiscent of the Buka.

"I don't want to disappear," I tell him.

"Mostly, I make *them* disappear!" He doffs his hat, and yet another dove flies forth and lands on my mother's bedpost, cooing.

"That's their mother, Mama Bird."

"She was under your hat!"

He pulls my earlobe and produces a shiny silver dollar.

"Things are hidden everywhere, if you know where to look," he says solemnly.

"Do you know where to look for my mother?" I blurt out, and even to me, my voice suddenly has an accusing tone.

A guilty look flickers across Leon's face. "You know"—he coughs nervously—"she had to go to the hospital."

"Can we visit?"

Leon looks very uncomfortable. "Your mother will be home"—he takes a breath—"on May thirtieth. It's only seven days."

"My birthday," I say. "I know you have a

phone number; I heard her give it to you. Can't we call her now?"

"She's sleeping," he says, "and you should be too . . . it's after midnight."

Leon knows more about my mother than I do, and he won't tell. I clutch my mother's bathrobe, wrapping it tightly around me. I can see her fluffy comforter, with the same rose pattern, folded on the edge of her bed.

"I want to take my mother's comforter to my room," I say.

Leon looks right into my eyes.

"Good idea," he says. I can't wait to wrap the comforter around me; I can already smell my mother's perfume and something less easy to define, her personal scent. Like vanilla.

"Here." Leon helps me adjust the comforter as an extra shawl, which trails after me.

"Listen, Zoya," Leon says. "I am not one for rules, but I think it would make a great deal of sense for you to go to bed now. Don't you?"

"I might go to bed, but I won't sleep." I tell him. "I won't sleep until my mother comes home." I want to ask him more, but I fear the answer. My mother said she was having "an exploratory"—she said that is when the doctor explores you to see if anything is wrong.

When he explored, did the doctor find something?

I can still hear my mother's reassurance before she left: "If they find anything, they will fix it. Do not worry."

CHAPTER FOUR

Mr. Uzzle and Spike

May 24, 7 A.M.

Sunlight. I hear the springtime sounds of birds chirping, inside and out. The light slants into my room. I look through my window at the banner of the bleaching sky. Pigeons are perching on the Stone Girl, and some are taking wing baths in the fountain.

Did I fall asleep? I have no sense of having slept, yet I feel odd, as if something happened last night. . . . I am missing pieces of the puzzle my life has become. . . . I am stiffened into position, still at my desk, wearing my red ruby shoes. Oddly, they look muddy. Could I have not noticed they were dirty?

Music is playing, and that excites Nicky, who is gripping his perch for support as he throws himself into a shrill harmony with the happy tune, a light rock song. Down the hall, the doves are cooing. Are the doves real or did I dream them? Was it all a nightmare? My mother leaving, my run through the hallway, the broken figurines, getting locked out . . .

"Breakfast!"

No nightmare. Leon.

"I'll be right out!" I call back. I jump into the shower and let the hot water wash away the last shred of night fear. "Everything will be all right," I tell myself. Only six more days. I feel my blood hum. *Everything feels different today.*

I set out my own clothes instead of my mother helping me choose. I decide I might as well clash. Orange and red remind me of my mother, so I wear an orange sweater and my favorite jeans, with turquoise socks, and then the red sequin *Wizard of Oz* shoes. Once again, I have half a hope that if I click my heels together and wish, my mother will be in the other room, instead of Leon, making breakfast. I wish I could hear her whisking eggs for French toast, our favorite. I miss the sound of her singing a little off-key ("I never said I could sing!") as she cooks.

Outside my bedroom door, I see more proof that I did not dream the events of last night: Gramma's china cabinet looks different. I peer into it and see the china boy, who used to bow, is broken. His head has snapped off, and he lies on the shelf. If Gramma sees this, it will be *my* head. Krazy Glue, I think. I will get into the cabinet before my mother returns, and glue the boy back together.

Leon listens to the radio as he fixes breakfast. He doesn't know we don't listen to rock or hip-hop—my mother likes jazz, classical, and her favorite is Louis Armstrong. This music has a fast beat, as if even the radio is picking up the tempo of change. Leon looks confusedly at the fridge, as if he can't find what he wants. "Are we cereal people or eggs?" he asks. "Do you drink coffee?"

"Not yet." I laugh. "The orange juice?" I

remind him. My mother squeezed a week's worth. I sit in the breakfast nook and suggest, "French toast or scrambled eggs?"

Leon says, "How about some fruit?"

I think of my mother, her brisk gestures with the fork, whisking the yellow eggs, dipping the bread in delicious batter.

"Watch this," Leon invites. And the next thing I know, he is tossing oranges and apples, juggling first two, then three, then four at a time. "I can't scramble," he confesses, "but I can juggle."

I peel a tangerine and eat a section at a time, being careful to unravel the white citrus threads and deposit the skins on my plate. "My mother always has flowers on the table," I say.

Leon flips his hand, and suddenly a bouquet is under my nose—not real flowers, but a bouquet of colored feathers!

I peel and nibble the sections of two tangerines. Leon drinks coffee, black, and eats a bagel. He gives me a bagel too, but I don't eat bagels; I tuck it into my backpack.

"I need lunch money," I say.

Leon reaches into his back pocket—he is wearing jeans and a sweater—and produces a wad of crisp twenties. He peels off a twenty-dollar bill and gives it to me.

My heart pounds—Wow! He knows nothing. Lunch is always $1.50 and my mother gives me a single and two quarters.

"Don't spend it all in one place," he says.

When I put on my windbreaker, I see Leon grab the keys and prepare to walk out the door of 2B with me. This is a little embarrassing—I had not planned to go out in public with him. "I'll walk you to school," he says, confirming my fears.

"I can go myself." My mother walks me, but what does he know?

"Your mother said to walk you," he says.

Okay, he knows. I wonder if he knows that we have the big seventh-grade spring dance a week from Saturday. The music teacher already took my name from my mother, so she is expecting me. I am worried no one will ask me to dance. Some of the girls are already going out. "I'm going in," I say. It's a joke my mother really gets.

"Yes," she says, "I went in a lot myself at twelve."

But she wants me to have more friends than she had when she was my age. "Everything is different now," she says. "It's easier for boys and girls to be friends, real friends."

Is it? I haven't found that to be the case.

And I am dreading this big spring dance. I hope she didn't tell Leon about it.

"And I know about the spring dance a week from Saturday," he says.

Oh no. He doesn't expect me to go with *him*? But my mother will be back by then, won't she?

I look at Leon and try to imagine how he will appear to the other kids at school. He is loping along, a seven-foot guy in jeans. He is old—at least forty. By the morning light, I see a zigzag of silver in his black hair, as if lightning made him turn gray, just at that one place. It's not that he looks bad; it's just that I find it weird to be seen with him.

I wonder if I can walk a little ahead of him and people won't realize we are together. I am already focusing on what Flynn, my only friend in the building, will say if she sees him with me.

I am hoping this day Flynn will wait up for me so we can walk together. That will neutralize Leon's being with me—it will look more like a normal day. If she is waiting for me, she will be outside at the great wrought-iron gate, the entry to our courtyard. But I can't count on Flynn. She seems to skip school more than she goes. I have never forgotten the first time I saw Flynn, with her one green and one brown eye and her black bangs. She was framed by the red curtains and a picture of a crystal ball above her head. I could see behind her to the glow of a lit television set, a tangle of plastic toys, and the two crawling toddlers. She didn't look away when I spotted her but held my gaze in a stare. The two different-colored eyes give her an unusual look, but to tell you the truth, from that first moment I spotted her, I always thought she looked pretty.

Flynn doesn't live in an apartment but in a storefront on the street side of Roxy's Mansion. Her mother is known as Mrs. Sheila and she has a sign in the window, PSYCHIC READER. Flynn's apartment doesn't have walls, only curtains—red-and-orange-patterned curtains with fringed blob shapes, like hairy amoebas. The curtains are not just in the window but also inside, as room dividers. Flynn and her mother are said to be Gypsies, and while I like the sound of Gypsies, our super, Mr. Uzzle, says *gyp* means "cheat" and comes from the word *Gypsy*.

Leon takes me downstairs to head for school. We see Flynn already outside in the courtyard. I have never been so happy to see her.

"Hey," she greets us. She is slamming a ball against the courtyard wall. Flynn always wears a striped polo shirt and jeans. Even in winter, she won't wear a coat. She has a big gray sweatshirt with a hood.

Flynn has so many freckles that they blend together like dots in a comic book. At a distance, she looks as if she has a tan.

She is punching the ball against the wall, and just as we get near, the ball hits the bottom window grate that is level with the basement, the super's window. There is an instant roar from down below.

"Gid outa here! Cut that out!" Mr. Uzzle screams. I look at Leon—is he ready to take this on? Mr. Uzzle hates Flynn and her family. He is always trying to "get them out." He says they don't keep the place nice, that they cause trouble, and that they eat worms and mice.

We are scared of Mr. Uzzle; he yells, "Get out of here," when we play in the courtyard. He is even meaner if you go down to the basement, to the laundry room.

Mr. Uzzle yells when he does his work—he heaves trash cans, mops the hall. He always makes a racket, slamming cans down; he kicks the walls and bangs the lids.

"I don't want you kids down here," he screams. Mr. Uzzle lives behind a metal gate he clangs shut, with his evil pit bull, Spike. All Mr. Uzzle really seems to want to do is squat down there in the basement and drink straight from a bottle ("Mr. Uzzle Likes to Guzzle" was a poem I once wrote) and watch his big color TV and smoke cigars. I secretly envy Mr. Uzzle the size of his TV—I can see it through the gate—because it is as big as a wall and there are always figures in black fighting and crashing cars.

We have interrupted his early-morning TV. Leon calls down to the grate, a tiny barred window at the level of our feet. Through the bars we can see a slice of the basement, and hear Spike growling and barking and Mr. Uzzle barking back.

Leon speaks up, in that polite formal way he has, without shouting.

"Sorry, the ball hit your window by accident."

We can see a little of Mr. Uzzle's face as he peers up from the basement. He has a big nose, gray but studded, like a strawberry, with a network of red tracings. His face always goes from gray to red, and I can see Mr. Uzzle is getting redder even through the cellar grating.

"Just wad I needed. I know who did it." He glares at Flynn and me. His eyes are small and red, like his dog's peeking through the grate.

"Hey," says Leon, stooping his long frame to address the slit eyes and the strawberry-studded nose. "It's an accident—we apologize for any inconvenience!"

"Do not," says Flynn. She rubs her sneaker

toe in the dirt. "I don't need anybody saying 'sorry' when I'm not," she tells Leon. "Nobody yells at me! Nobody tells me what to do! I do what I want!"

"So do I!" Leon tells her, taking her by surprise.

Flynn starts to laugh, but then she covers her mouth with her hand. It's a gesture she has, to hide her teeth, which have a pitted look.

My mother gets a kick out of Flynn. According to Mimi, Flynn is smart and exotic; she has "hybrid vigor." Hybrid is when you cross plants and the result is a stronger baby plant. Flynn, being from two different cultures—Irish and Gypsy—has the best of both. Her full name is Flynn O'Reilly Radescu.

"Just don't go around saying 'sorry' for me when I'm not," she says to Leon.

"Sorry," he says, grinning.

"Not," she says, but she flashes her gray smile, quick, before hiding her teeth with her hand again.

"Are you coming to school with us?" she asks him.

"Yeah," he says, matching her tough way, but smiling. "Any problem with that?"

"Well," she says, her hands on her hips, "I don't know that I'm going to school today."

"Oh, please," I beg. She just has to go to school today.

"There's funny stuff going on around the building; I think maybe I better stay home and investigate," Flynn says.

Did she hear the strange cries from the basement last night too?

"I heard weird sounds," she says, "in the basement under me. Somebody, something . . ."

"Was crying," I finish for her.

"And now I come out here, and look at that!"

I follow her pointing finger—the Stone Girl!

I wonder, did she see it too? Did she witness the transformation last midnight? When it seemed, at least to me, that the Stone Girl shivered?

I am almost afraid to look at the Stone Girl by the hard morning light. But I do, and when I see her, I gasp. The statue is wearing a blanket, a fuzzy pale blanket. Someone covered her last night. Even at a distance, I recognize the cloth—it's my Mickey. How did my blanket get out to the courtyard?

I am too stunned and embarrassed to claim it, but Flynn marches over and yanks the blanket off the statue. She looks at me, her different-colored eyes questioning. My mind spins. Maybe somebody stole my blanket and placed it over the Stone Girl?

As if on cue, the Disgusting Boy slinks out of the archway; he has been watching us and the statue. The Disgusting Boy is our least favorite boy in the school. His real name is Eugene. He really *is* disgusting—he wipes his nose on his sleeve, which always looks crusted. I glare at him. One time, right after I moved here, he chased me down the street, yelling, "You have no dad! You have no dad!" He should know better, because he has no mom. He lives with his dad in our building, and everyone knows his mother left them. His eyes follow me. I turn away. I really hate the Disgusting Boy.

I glare at him: *I know you did it!* But then I

remember the mud on my red shoes.

I want to claim the Mickey—I have to—but even in front of Flynn, I'm embarrassed.

Leon reaches out to Flynn and his big hand closes over the Mickey. He throws me a look, as if to say "Don't worry, this secret is safe with me."

"Please go to school," I say to her. "I want you to go with me."

Flynn hesitates.

Leon starts toward the gates, heading out toward the school.

"Come on, girls." He turns. "I don't want you young ladies to be late."

"We're not young ladies," Flynn says, but she falls into step, thank goodness. We walk under the arch. "We're going down to the basement right after school," she hisses. "I want to know who is crying down there."

Our eyes meet. We share the need to know.

We walk just behind Leon. The junior high school is only a block away, but it is a steep block. The neighborhood is on a slant, and the long street slides down toward the river. As we walk, we pass other buildings like Roxy's Mansion—all named and gated, big buildings, with their giant soot-darkened faces.

I see my school, redbrick and square. My mother is always saying how lucky we were to get Gramma's apartment, in this great neighborhood and in a good school district.

Leon hesitates at the gate, as if he is wondering whether to kiss me good-bye. I think of my mother, always here, always with her happy send-off—"Later, later, Sweetheart," and the kiss she blows in the air. I am stunned when Leon leans toward me—he is not going to kiss me! And he doesn't. To my shock, he does something even more strange—he reaches out and shakes my hand.

"À bientôt," he says, which I know is French for "See you soon."

I wonder if Flynn finds him weird. But her green and brown eyes are each sparkling. "He may turn out to be really cool," she says.

"He is going to show me magic," I tell her.

"Show me, too," she says.

School is only an intermission to the ongoing

drama at Roxy's Mansion. By unspoken consent, I meet Flynn outside at three, after dismissal, and we race back to the building. I am almost afraid to look at the Stone Girl, but we do look and I see something new that makes me gasp—lying in the base of her fountain is a tiny bird's eggshell, cracked and bright blue. A poor bulge-eyed embryo, the robin that would never be, is stretched out. His dried feathers are caked with egg; he was smashed in his own shell. Poor bird, I think, you never got to splash in the fountain or fly. You never got to live at all.

"Oh, Flynn!" I cry.

"It's an omen," she says, solemn. "We can ask my mother what it means, but I bet I already know—something terrible is going to happen! Dead birds lead to dead people! That's the way it is."

"My mother!" I silently scream. I look up at the Stone Girl, as if she could comfort me. After all, she witnessed everything last night. She knows all the secrets—who cries in the basement, who killed the little bird in its shell.

I feel we should not leave the little dead bird

where it is, and Flynn agrees. She manages to dig a hole in the earth under the fountain, and we set the tiny body there and cover it with dirt and a big loose stone. As we dig, I can't resist confiding in Flynn how many mysterious things have been happening since my mother left, and how I am keeping a diary. "I am still trying to find my first memory," I admit, "and it is just out of reach. . . . I know it is important, but maybe I will never really remember."

"Well, I remember mine!" Flynn says. "I remember being born! I just dove out of there and surprised everyone. I remember seeing light! I came from the red cavern. My next memory is climbing out of the damned crib—I hit the floor running! No bars can hold me! I can even remember my life *before*!"

I cannot suppress a "Wow." Flynn is cool; no wonder she is so brave. "What was your life before?" I ask.

"I was a boy," she confesses, "a pirate! They tried to hang me, but I used the rope as a swing!"

Just then, who comes along but the Disgusting

Boy. He stands watching, and I have a real fear he will dig up the bird when we are gone.

"Come on," I whisper to Flynn. "Let's get out of here."

Our eyes meet, and I can see even Flynn is scared to go down in the basement, but we are determined. The Disgusting Boy moves, like he is following.

"Where are you going?" he asks.

"None of your business," Flynn says real tough, and spits—not directly at the Disgusting Boy, but near him. The Disgusting Boy backs off. "And don't you dare follow us!" Flynn warns.

Flynn and I have a mission. We must find out who or what was crying last night.

Trying not to make a sound, we enter the service door to reach the basement level, and there is the mesh gate, unlocked but shut. I push, and it swings inward.

"I don't hear anything," whispers Flynn.

We stand, concentrating. Then I do hear it—the weak crying. The cries are plaintive, sad, seducing me farther down the hall. Who or what could be pleading like this? Whimpering and moaning?

The sounds grow louder; I feel I am closer, when the light, already dim down below, flickers—not blacking out, but hesitating. In the darkness, the crying stops, but I hear another sound behind me, and I turn into the electric orb of a flashlight aimed directly into my eyes.

"Whad are you doin' down here?" a voice yells.

My only answer is a reflexive uncontrolled scream. A hand clamps over my mouth, and I hear a whisper in my ear. "Sssssh!" Flynn hisses.

"What did I say about the basement?" Mr. Uzzle is yelling. Then, almost in another language, the language of the basement—"Gid outa here!"

Flynn and I race, our hearts pounding, back up to her home in the storefront. We tear through the curtains, the door that says MRS. SHEILA. PSYCHIC READER.

Flynn's mother, Mrs. Sheila, looks up when we enter. Although the other mothers do not like Mrs. Sheila, I am really glad to see her. She seems like a permanent exhibit, in a recliner in front of the TV, reliable in an exhausted way. Mrs. Sheila is nodding off, and she snorts when she sees us—"Nuh? You want something to eat? We're having bologna and macaroni tonight."

Mrs. Sheila seems too fatigued to rise. Unlike Flynn, whose ribs show through her shirt, Mrs. Sheila is plump with a behind like a great continental shelf.

"You want a soda?" she invites. She gestures toward the refrigerator, which stands behind another curtain.

"Can you tell my fortune?" I ask.

"Well," she answers, "I have the gift."

"How much to know the future?" I ask.

"How much have you got?" she asks, but in a way I sense is habit; and I'm right, for she waves her hand as if to say "Eh, who cares about the money?" and says, "Let me see your palm, honey. . . ."

I hold out my palm and she looks at it, long and hard.

"Where is my mother, and is she really

coming back?" I ask. I hear my voice shake.

Mrs. Sheila has red hair, too, like my mother, but Mrs. Sheila's has a white stripe down her center part, and a funny tint, not ginger like my mother's. She bends over my palm, so I am studying her hair up close, and I suspect her hair is white with red dye on it, and that is the reason for the stripe, and the pale pink color.

She looks up at me, and her eyes are weak blue, with little beads of flesh that hang like permanent tears on the eyelids.

Her eyes turn, tightening like a kaleidoscope, colors changing, and I sense a shiver—from her to me, and in that shiver is some terrible truth she doesn't want to share. She must see me go pale and sway. My night without sleep is catching up with me.

"Who is crying in the basement?" I ask quickly, so she will not have to answer my first question.

"Yeah," agrees Flynn, "who is crying night and day down there?"

"You'll find out" is her only answer to both questions. She looks deeply into my eyes, and this time there is no shiver but just the shade of a smile.

CHAPTER FIVE

Dear Mimi

May 24, 5 P.M.

At dinner Leon appeared with a rotisserie chicken in a bag. We sat in the breakfast nook, Leon in my mother's chair. He placed his magic feather bouquet in an empty vase, and then he lit candles as my mother would have done.

My mother always says: "It isn't so much what you eat as how you eat it." She insists on "a little ceremony." Flowers, candles, what she calls "atmosphere." Sometimes she spends more money on flowers and candles than on food. She makes omelets a lot, and thin pancakes she calls crepes, which she stuffs with a different filling every night. I like the creamy chicken crepes the best.

"This chicken is greasy," I say. "My mother would not buy this chicken."

"Do you want pizza? I can order one," Leon offers.

"I am sick of pizza," I say, imitating my mother, who says, "If I see one more pizza, I will move to Italy for a really good one!"

"Well," Leon says, "what would you like?"

"Crepes filled with creamy chicken filling, and cherries jubilee. My mother makes me that. Can we call her now? Before dinner?"

Leon says, "All right. Let's try."

He punches in the buttons on the kitchen phone. I hold my breath. *Please, please,* I pray, *let me hear her voice. . . .*

Leon is saying my mother's name, and a room number. He speaks to someone. "She's asleep," he says.

Already? I think.

"Tomorrow," he promises. So in the meantime, I direct him to the fridge and the stove. Leon's crepes are thicker than my mother's, but she left the chicken filling, so they taste pretty good. He is challenged by the cherries jubilee.

"They have to flame," I say, "but I don't know how my mother does it."

"Rum?" he asks, then pours himself a small glass and drinks it in one gulp.

We eat nonflambéed cherries jubilee—just cherries on ice cream. But to make up for the lack of fire, Leon demonstrates a new trick. He does what he calls Fingers of Fire! He waves and suddenly he is holding a candelabra, fully ablaze, in one hand.

I am close enough to him, in the breakfast nook, to see he has a metal brace over his hand that actually holds the candles.

"I know the secret!" I cry. "So now can I become a magician too?"

"Are you ready to take the Magician's Oath?"

"That I can never tell the secrets?" I ask. "Not even to Flynn or my mother when she comes home?"

"Not to anyone who is not a certified magician."

I hesitate.

"You're not ready," he says, his voice kind. "Maybe later in the week."

May 25, midnight

I hate myself a little for what I have to do tonight when Leon falls asleep. But I cannot help it—I have to know more about Leon, more about my mother, more about everything that has been kept hidden from me. I am thinking I must make another try to get my little plaid suitcase, the one I carried from Russia when I was four years old.

When the clock chimes midnight, I sneak out of my room, and I hear Leon mutter, but I know he is fast asleep.

I am barefoot, tiptoeing. I have to take off my mother's bathrobe, so I don't trip this time. And forget standing on that wobbly chair. I am going to try climbing the stepladder to the top of the hall closet. If I pull the light cord in the closet, the Buka will stay hidden and not pounce on me.

I creep into the kitchen, find the stepladder, and drag it to the hall closet. I can hear Leon breathing deeply behind my mother's bedroom door.

In the midnight darkness, I climb the ladder, determined to reach the highest shelf. I yank the cord—and in the nick of time! A black shadow was reaching forward as if to seize my hand! As the light hits, the shadow pulls back. I struggle with the suitcase, but I still can't get a good grip on the leather handle.

I scramble down and move quickly, tense in my need to remain quiet, as I replace the stepladder in the kitchen. I take pliers from the whatnot drawer and return to my room. If I can't get the suitcase, I can at least crack open the letter box I found last night.

Nicky chirps as I enter. Even Natalie seems to twitch. We are all in this together. I reach under the bed and drag out the clear plastic letter box, then set it on my writing desk.

Should I read the letters? I think of how upset I would be if someone read my diary.

But this is different, I think. *I need to know the facts.*

I crack the lock.

The letters are grouped in separate bundles, tied with ribbon. I see they are gathered by the years stamped on the envelopes. I note the dates are long before my birth. And immediately I see Leon's name on the return addresses. So he was writing to my mother, letters that she saved.

"My darling Mimi," I begin to read.

As if on cue, I hear a cry. From far, far below. The cry is coming from the vent—I am sure of it.

I crouch down on the floor and listen. Yes, it is that same distressed whimpering. I try to ignore it. What can I do? I can't go back down there, not with Mr. Uzzle and Spike on the prowl. I rise, sit back at my desk, and try to concentrate on the letters. . . .

"My darling Mimi," I read, "I am wondering if you gave my last letter some thought. You know how I feel about you, and I sense you care for me also. . . ."

I lift the page, and a glossy black-and-white photograph falls onto the floor. I turn it over, and see—my mother looks so beautiful, so sure of herself . . . but so young! She must be a teenager in these pictures. There she is again—levitating, in a sparkly costume!

Now I hear another sound, a *tap tap* on the front door of 2B. Who could this be? In the middle of the night?

I look out the window and check the Stone Girl. She stands, glazed with moonlit rain sheeting over her thinly dressed form.

Tap. Tap. Tap.

I walk to the front door. My heart is beating so fast, I can see my nightgown move above my chest.

"It's me," I hear Flynn whisper from the other side of the door. "I found her."

I open the door. Flynn is standing there, covered in soot. She is so dirty, I cannot see her freckles, only the sparkle in her eyes.

"Come quickly. I need your help!"

I grab my coat and pull it over my nightgown, remembering this time to take my keys.

"We have to hurry." Flynn leads me down the DO NOT ENTER EMERGENCY EXIT ONLY! stairs.

"What about Mr. Uzzle? What about Spike?"

"It'll be okay," Flynn tells me.

I am shaking, but I must know who is crying. Flynn leads me, and I take courage from her. She is afraid of nothing, not Mr. Uzzle or his dog, Spike. She doesn't know about the Buka, but I bet even that would not scare Flynn.

"Watch this," she says, and shows me a handful of bologna. "I already gave the dog some; he loves it."

Spike by day is a fearsome creature: that pink face, the blinking white eyelashes. But in the night, Spike surprises me by being gentle; he laps first at the bologna with his pink tongue, then at Flynn's hand.

He looks at us in obvious dog gratitude. He lets us pass without barking.

Flynn leads me down the basement hall. "There is a tunnel here. This is where she is hiding."

All around us in the cellar are sounds of machinery and heat—pipes hiss and motors grumble.

I feel as if I am in the hold of a great ship; these are the engines that pump fizzing steam and conduct heat to our apartments upstairs. We pass rows of fuse boxes, each with an apartment number. There are storage zones, gated and closed, and finally, I see it—a narrow tunnel that begins at knee level.

"She's in there."

Flynn produces a flashlight; I recognize it as the one Mr. Uzzle used on us.

"I swiped it," she says with a grin.

We crouch, and she aims the flashlight into the tunnel. I peer inside.

The cries, which had been faint, suddenly stop.

"She's scared," explains Flynn.

Then I see, in the reflection of the flashlight, two bright eyes, black with red dots in the centers. Is there a demon living deep in the hole? The red-dot gaze does not flinch.

Flynn calls softly, "It's all right, we're here to

save you. . . . Come out and we'll give you something to eat."

Flynn assures me. "She's coming; she's just scared. She needs this bologna."

She holds up a second package.

I can smell its spicy scent.

I hear a small scratchy sound, as if something is making its way toward the entry of the tunnel; the red dots loom larger, and then change to golden green.

And then I see her.

The cat.

She is gray, covered in dirt. Her mouth opens and a pink tongue flicks out. She is so scared, she is afraid to take the meat from Flynn's hand. She backs away, but she is so starved, she cannot resist. She darts foward and hungrily tears at the pink meat.

The cat has fine pointy ears and a pointy chin, but she is so thin, her shoulder bones show and even some of her ribs. Her belly bulges out, as if she has swallowed a football.

"I think," pronounces Flynn, "she is about to have kittens!"

Flynn fills me in on the story of this cat, a stray that has been hiding in the basement. Mr. Uzzle has already called an exterminator.

"I heard him say they will pump poison gas into her tunnel," Flynn tells me. "That's why we have to save her tonight!"

CHAPTER SIX

Playful

"I named her Playful," Flynn says. "Look. . . ."

Flynn is rubbing the little cat under the chin, and the cat hisses and arches her back. She doesn't look very playful to me.

"You'll see," Flynn says. "She's just scared."

The cat gives another awful hiss and freezes sideways, in the traditional Halloween cat arched-back pose. She shows her pearly white fangs.

"Listen, Playful," Flynn says in a strict voice I have never heard her use. "We're here to save your life."

The cat seems to listen; she eats more bologna, and then Flynn shows me she has also brought the cat a little square container of chocolate milk from the school lunch.

"Will a cat drink chocolate milk?" I ask, but before the words are out of my mouth, Playful is pushing her nose into the ripped-open container and licking, lick after swift pink lick.

"This one likes chocolate milk," Flynn says.

"We must hide her," Flynn tells me, "and my mother says we can't keep her at my place."

She looks at me. "You know what you have to do," she says. The cat issues her first loud purr, competing with the mechanical sounds of the cellar.

"I don't know what Leon will say," I tell her.

"We have to try."

She hands Playful to me. She is dirty, but soft and warm; she seems to settle into my arms, and I can feel her big belly, with its inner life; the poke of what I imagine are tiny kitten feet.

Oh, I am thinking, *my mother and I always wanted little kittens.*

We return the same way we entered, this time with Playful in my arms.

When I get to my door, Flynn says, "Well, do you want me to come in with you for good luck?"

I think that is a good idea—there is power in numbers.

I try to be quiet, but before I can finish twisting the knob, the door swings inward and I see Leon holding it from the other side.

He is wearing striped pajamas and a windbreaker.

"Thank God," he greets us. "I've been scared to death."

Good start, I think. He is so relieved that I have come home, he may not object to the cat.

Flynn explains how the cat was crying, and she is doomed unless we hide her. "The super will poison her. We have to save her!"

Leon nods, and asks what my mother would say in a case like this.

"Oh," I assure him, "she would definitely want Playful. She would make a nice box for her, and let me hide her in my own bathroom. I know she would. . . ."

He looks undecided.

"Please," Flynn and I say together.

I see Leon is studying Flynn, and now I look at her too. She really looks pretty dirty, and her nose has started to run.

"Jeez," Leon says, half under his breath, "I never saw this coming."

He helps fold an old towel into a cardboard box.

"Maybe in the bathtub, so she stays safe," he suggests.

I am thinking I wish my mother could see this. We have a menagerie now—Leon's three doves, the new cat, Nicky. . . .

For the first time since my mother disappeared, I feel an emotion that is not pure pain.

"Everything will be okay," Leon says. "I have a feeling it's a good sign."

"It can't be wrong to save a life, even a cat life," I encourage him. "And you're not just saving one cat," I say, to add to his good feeling.

"You have saved her babies, too."

"Yeah," he says anxiously, "and I wonder how many babies there will be. . . ."

"There could be a whole bunch," I tell him.

"I saw a cat with nine!" Flynn says.

"I better walk you downstairs," he offers to Flynn.

"Oh, I can go myself," she says.

Leon looks undecided. He is really new to this. "I'll be right back," he tells me. "I'll take Flynn home. You might think about getting into bed."

I like how he puts things—he never says, "You better do this! Do it now! Because I said so!"

He lets me consider what he calls "the alternatives."

"If you stay up later, you'll be really tired, and maybe this way, we'll have time to get some supplies for Playful in the morning," he adds.

I am heading toward my bed when I realize—the love letters! I left the bundles on my desk. I look at my desk—everything is gone: the see-through plastic box, the pliers, and the letters themselves.

There is a blue silk ribbon lying on my blotter, fallen from the first bundle.

When I pick up the ribbon, I see there is a note tucked on top of my unlocked diary:

> I wouldn't read your diary, so please don't read my letters. —Leon.
>
> P.S. I need a new assistant in my magic act. Do you think you could be ready to perform in a few days?

Suddenly, Leon is there in the doorway. "Your mother is on the phone . . ."

I run so fast that I trip on the doorsill and fall onto Leon.

"She's fine," he says, "but don't tire her."

I grab the phone. "It's me!" I cry. "I miss you so much! Can you come home sooner? Tonight!"

I hear my mother sigh on the other end. Her voice when she speaks sounds faint and faraway as she whispers she loves me, and will return on my birthday.

"Not sooner?"

My mother is murmuring, in that small voice, from so far off, that she will keep her promise, and not to worry. I hear her make a faint kissing noise.

"Are you keeping the diary?" she whispers.

"Yes, and so much is happening!" I want to tell her about the suspicious sounds, the shadows, Playful and the Stone Girl . . . but instead, I blurt out, "I think it's time to look inside the suitcase!" Silence. Of course she knows what suitcase I mean. Is she angry I am asking when she has so many other worries?

Leon takes the phone quietly and talks for a moment before saying good-bye. "She has to rest," he explains. "She says it's fine for you to open the suitcase as long as you're ready for what you will find inside. She wants to know everything when she gets back—about the cat, and now . . . the magic act." His eyes look me over. "I have a job at the Black Hat nightclub. I need a new Sonambula." I hesitate.

"Do I get to wear the gold costume, the crown, and the cape?"

He answers my question with another: "Are you ready to take the oath?"

CHAPTER SEVEN

White Night

May 26, 7 P.M.

Leon takes my hand and holds it over an old maroon leather book with symbols on the cover. I cannot repeat, even in the privacy of this diary, the exact Magicians' Oath, because part of the oath is that you must never repeat it to a nonmagician. I tell you only that I swore my loyalty to the Society of Magicians, and we rehearsed all afternoon, and into Sunday.

Some tricks are harder than others, and I am not sure I will be good in the act, but there is no time to waste.

• • •

I wear my mother's makeup, because I look a little pale without it for stage work. I cannot believe my own reflection in the mirror—a true Sonambula!

The costume is four sizes too large, but Leon says he will fix that for the show. I should just concentrate on my role.

I'm pretty good, rehearsing in our living room, but will I remember my complicated moves in front of an audience? Under the cape I will wear a sparkling leotard, and on my head a jeweled and feathered tiara headdress. THE ASTOUNDING ARMAND AND SONAMBULA. MORE THAN MAGIC—MIRACLES AND ILLUSIONS.

"I might get stage fright," I tell Leon. I forgot my lines last year in the class play. I was a Colonial housewife, and I was supposed to scream, "The Revolution has begun! To arms!" and I could not remember the words. I just stood onstage, with a Colonial hat and apron, and yelled, "It's the revolution!" and ran off. My mother said I was great anyway, that I gave a good impression of panic at wartime. "What will I have to do when we are actually onstage?" I ask Leon. "Will I disappear?"

"Definitely not. It's easy—you have talent, I can tell. Just remember what I show you." Then, suddenly, from under his cloak he produces the secret box with his and my mother's letters. My face burns. Is he going to punish me?

"It was locked and hidden, so it drove me crazy," I confess. "I just had to see what was inside."

"Then see," Leon orders, slowly lifting the lid.

I am staring at a glossy black-and-white photograph of Leon, the Astounding Armand, but he is much younger. His face is even skinnier than it is now, and his Adam's apple pokes up even more. He looks like a teenager, and there is a pretty girl in a feathered costume with a crown standing next to him—"The first Sonambula!"

Even though the picture was taken long ago, I recognize my mother. She looks very glamorous in a feather boa, and she is holding out her hand with a white dove perched on her finger. My mother was the first Sonambula! My mother and Leon knew each other as teenagers; they started the act—The Amazing Armand and Sonambula—together.

"Sonambula," I say. "That means . . ."

Leon gives me his kindest look; his eyes soften. "Sonambula means . . . sleepwalker."

Perfect casting, I think. Then I wonder, *Was my mother a sleepwalker?*

Later that night, or is it morning?

Alone in my room, I rock back and forth, hugging my knees as I whisper the story my mother Mimi always tells—of my birth and adoption. I can almost hear her voice:

"I found you when you were four years old—and that was the new start to both our lives. I wanted a child, and when I saw you, in the hospital in Russia, it was love at first sight. . . . I don't know why it happened this way, but I truly believe our meeting was meant to be. You and me."

Yet I can remember voices other than my mother's soft, gentle one. I can still hear Gramma: "Women should have children when they have a home and a husband of their own. You don't know what you are taking on—a child like that; it could be trouble. No one knows who she is really. . . . She is not a baby; four is too old to adopt. You should have taken a baby. There will be something wrong with her. You don't know her heredity."

I didn't know what that word meant—*heredity*—when I was four. I thought heredity was a specific quality, like red hair. My mother always corrects Gramma and anyone who asks, "Is that your *real* daughter?" or "Who are her *real* parents?" My mother has a soft voice, but she sounds sharp when she shoots back—"Zoya is my *real* daughter; I am her *real* mother."

But of course I am curious, too, have always been curious about that other mother, the two people my mother is careful to call my "birth parents."

Until now, I have imagined them as fuzzy

blank people in Russia, standing side by side at my birth. I don't picture that first mother giving birth, only attending my birth, because her role was so soon finished.

I see those parents almost as a bride and groom at the altar of my delivery. Being there for the birth, but not ever after. "Did they leave right away as soon as I was born?" I once asked my mother.

"You were meant to be with me," my mother said.

And she told, over and over again, how she fell in love with me when I was already four, and alone in what she calls "the hospital" and Gramma calls "the orphanage."

I know from books and movies that orphanages were buildings that held lost children who slept in rooms lined with cots, wore aprons, mopped floors, and sometimes sang about wanting to leave and have a real home and real parents of their own. Orphans were children whose parents had died, or, for some reason, were missing.

I cannot remember if my orphanage was like that. All I remember are these flashes—the green crib, the icicles, and the sound of someone moaning. My mother made "the hospital" sound a little nicer, like a sunny yellow dormitory, where children got to go home with nice new mothers and fathers who came to pick them up and take them home—forever.

My mother always tells the story this way—

"I walked into the playroom and there you were, in a little black-checked dress and wearing a red kerchief. Your back was to me and you were playing with your doll. When you heard my step, you turned and looked at me. You looked sad, and then you looked up at me with your beautiful brown eyes and—you smiled. I never saw such a smile. And that was that!"

Then she tells the part about our Big Trip home.

"We held hands all the way on the flight to America."

I like this part of the story. I can say it by heart—

"We held hands for ten hours straight . . ."

"All the way," she confirms.

"We didn't even let go to eat dinner—we held our silverware with the opposite hands."

We always observe a funny little pause then, and I know in that pause is a lot more information, the secrets of my birth and the other events that occurred on that first trip together. But my mother and I have an unspoken agreement; there are things we don't discuss. I can see into her eyes, though, and I know—we both remember; we are thinking of the same moments; we have just chosen to cut out what is too sad or too scary. Tears spring to my eyes and I sit down on my bed, the plaid suitcase beside me. Leon took it down from the closet for me and left it on my bed.

Gently I open it. There is a note inside from my mother. "When you read this, you will be old enough to understand. I was able to tell you only part of this story when you were little. Now you are becoming a young woman, and you have every right to see this and know the truth. There is no way I could love you, my darling daughter, more than I do. Later, later, Sweetheart. Your mother, Mimi." And then I see that small checked dress, the red kerchief, and a tiny pair of shoes.

I am shocked at the force of my crying. I cry silently, my fist jammed into my mouth in some awful remembered way.

Why? I am crying inside. *Why was I taken away?*

Under the clothing there is a stack of smeary documents with official-looking seals.

I shut the lid. I am not ready to learn more. Not tonight.

Sometimes, I view my life like an outtake from *The Wizard of Oz*. Like Dorothy, I crash-landed here, and the world went from black and white to color. To my own surprise, tonight I am not ready to rewind this film and return to the grainy black-and-white world I see hidden inside this suitcase.

• • •

I lie down fully dressed on my bed and immediately enter the white world of a remembered dream. The whiteness is profound, and in my dream—or is this a memory?—I wake and look out the window.

The window is not the window at Roxy's Mansion, but another window in another country. The street outside is bathed in moonlight; this is a magical night. The tree outside my window is filled with blossoms, and I know from their heavy scent that it is midnight, when they release their perfume.

This is summer in St. Petersburg, the long-forgotten city of my birth, in the season that knows no real night. I was born in summer, in the nightless time, and I knew only iridescence, until, somehow, everything went black and wrong.

In the dream, through this window, I recognize the white nights, the northern rainbow-hued lights that dance, as graceful as my Stone Girl but in perpetual flickering motion, like the light that danced in the living room that feverish afternoon when, for one brief moment, I knew the Secret of Life.

The beginning, then, was beautiful and bathed in white light until something—what?—blanketed me in darkness. Again, I feel my trembling fall, not to sleep, but to the basement of Roxy's Mansion, the dark territory of the Buka.

I wake and lie in bed, gasping. Is it night or day?

In the darkness, I wander from my room searching for the white light of my first memory—my point of view. I glide like a phantom down the hall, past my mother's door, and out the main entry of 2B. Through a veil, I see the dogwood tree outside and the Stone Girl smiling at me.

I am outside, at midnight, but have no true idea how I got there . . . I cannot recall taking the elevator or the stairs. The night wind whips my robe and dandelion fluff swirls around my head. Am I alive or dead?

I am Sonambula, the sleepwalker.

Mrs. Sheila's voice echoes in my head.

"Sometimes the strangest person you know is yourself," she once said to me.

In the morning, when I wake from a nearly sleepless white night, there are flower petals on my bed.

CHAPTER EIGHT

Sonambula

May 27, 7 A.M.

Again, sunshine, daylight, and Leon banish the phantoms of my troubled night. I find him sewing at the kitchen table. He has attached more hot pink and purple feathers to my costume to disguise the fact that it is too large for me. I run and get my magic Dorothy sequin shoes. I put on the costume, and Leon crowns me with the diamond-and-feather tiara.

Now I want more than anything to succeed in the act. I will not spill Leon's secrets, but I will say here in my diary, where I tell only the truth, that the assistant does more than the magician sometimes. The doves don't appear from the air or even from under Leon's hat (they would poop on his head, he says). That's why they wear funny harnesses.

All day we practice to recorded music, and I learn the wide gestures with the feather fans and scarves that hide what Leon must do to make objects and birds appear and disappear. One part I really love is the Zombie—a ball that I hide under a scarf. Leon waves a wand, and the Zombie rises in the air to music. Leon plays the music for this. The song is "A Summer Place."

Leon's own specialty is the Dancing Cane. Leon dances with the magical cane, and then it dances on its own. Even I don't know how he does this, and he is a great dancer, very graceful. I try to dance too, but I feel clumsy.

"You're fine," Leon says, but when it is time to leave for the nightclub, my heart pounds and I think maybe I am too scared to go. I can't help it, but my feet, in the red sparkly Dorothy shoes, seem rooted to the floor. Only Flynn knows what to do.

"You've got to include Nicky in the act!" she

says. We hide our new secret assistant from Leon and swear to smuggle him in Flynn's backpack into the Black Hat.

And that is how, for the first time in history, a cockatiel replaces a dove in a magic act. I am happy, thinking of Nicky in a little swing under my cape. He always feels warm and comforting, and I know what a good performer he is. He doesn't even need makeup with his two big orange circles, like rouge, on his cheeks.

A taxicab, yellow in the night, arrives for us, and Leon and I, with our concealed doves, and Flynn, hiding Nicky, are driven downtown to the neon edge of the city, where the stage is still empty, for our rehearsal. By eight o'clock, men and women sit at tables with pink and green drinks.

Leon gets up onstage and stretches his arm out to me. I stand behind the curtain, hiding Laverne under my cape.

Leon introduces me to the crowd, "I want you to meet my new assistant—Sonambula!" The recorded music plays, and I do as I have been taught. At the signal, I let the doves loose, and it looks like they've come from Leon's hat! I stand near the front cabaret table, and Flynn is waiting for my hand signal. She is hiding Nicky under her arm for the finale. I am a little scared—the lights shine on me, and the audience sits in the darkness. What if I fail?

All goes well until at the big music cue for the candelabra trick, I miss a beat. I must keep the details a secret, but it is my fault what happens next. The timing is off by a few seconds, and Leon's candle fingers ignite. His whole hand appears in flame! I scream and rush forward, taking off my cape to smother the fire. As I dive into Leon, Flynn mistakes my move for the signal and tosses Nicky to me, in a trick harness. My bird falls to the stage floor like a trussed duck. To make it worse, the little cockatiel screams! His wings are tied.

I freeze in place, unable to help Leon or my bird. Laverne takes flight and soars over the audience, pooping wildly in her excitement. Only MacDougall keeps his cool, sitting on a perch and watching the spectacle.

The audience screams, then laughs. I run

from the stage, holding the trussed Nicky. Leon, thinking fast, plunges his hand into a pitcher of ice water. I think I hear a sizzle. And I do hear Leon's gasp of shock as he spots Nicky. "Good Lord!" he yells.

What if he is seriously burned?

In the club the audience is muttering. Ducking backstage, Leon says, "Stay cool." He waves to the light and sound man and new music plays. He produces the Dancing Cane, and I watch the long walking stick rise, as if in thin air. Graceful as ever, Leon emerges, dancing with the cane, and the audience applauds.

But not for me. I am now a hunched bundle of misery in the dressing room and refuse to come out for the curtain call or bow.

"It's not your fault," Leon whispers when he finds me there. "My hand is okay. I got it in the cold water just in time." He even laughs. "That was an act they won't see again—the Five Flaming Fingers!"

He unties Nicky's harness, and thank goodness the cockatiel is angry but unhurt. He bites down hard on Leon's good hand.

What a disaster. I have failed. My debut as Sonambula is a complete failure.

As we ride back to Roxy's Mansion, we sit together in the back of the taxi, and I fall asleep, my head on Leon's shoulder. The next thing I remember is Leon whispering in my ear—"Sonambula, you might want to wake up; we're home." We drop Flynn off at the storefront. She disappears into the red glow inside.

Maybe it is because I am so sleepy, but the truth pops out of my mouth, like a hidden bird in the act: "You know where my mother is, and I want her back!" And I cry.

Leon looks helpless and just keeps saying, "Everything will be all right, everything will be all right."

A slashing rain has started, drenching the Stone Girl. As we walk into Roxy's Mansion, I am soaked through, and it is impossible to say whether it is rain or tears streaking my face.

CHAPTER NINE

Black Shoes

May 28, midnight

Before we even enter 2B, we know something unexpected has happened: A pair of black shoes, heavy, sad, and wet, has been set outside the door. The shoes are not alone; they are matched by a heavy black umbrella, opened and dripping. The shoes and the umbrella have been laid on a spread-out newspaper with the incongruous name of *Palm Beach Life*.

Gramma!

She is here. She has returned to Roxy's Mansion at the worst possible time.

For a wild moment, Leon and I exchange glances. "I don't want to go in!" I cry.

I think of Gramma and all her admonitions, warnings not to touch this or touch that. I can only begin to imagine how angry she will be to come here and find her daughter, my mother Mimi, replaced by this seven-foot magician, a cat in the bathtub, and three dove boxes in her former bedroom. Not to mention the decor. And the shattered china figure of the boy.

"We painted everything pink, violet, and green," I whisper to Leon as he turns the key in the lock. "I broke the figurine."

We enter, and the silence and dark assail me, like the Buka of old. I realize, of course, that Gramma never liked the lights on; she did not like waste of any kind. "The electric, the electric," she used to mutter, walking around the apartment tugging every light cord my mother and I had pulled for illumination.

She is sitting there in the darkness, in the monster chair. She has removed the slipcover, hot pink and lavender, that my mother created to disguise the griffin-footed, clawed throne.

"So," she says simply, in the darkness.

Leon and I, wet, hold the dove carriers, and the cases with all the magic equipment stand dripping on the foyer rug.

"So," she says again, accusingly.

So? I want to scream.

"So how are you?" Leon asks.

I take it he recognizes Gramma from some long-ago encounter.

"You," she greets him.

"Yes," he says. "Me."

"The Astounding Armand," she says, firing the syllables like bullets.

"At your service," he says, and I can tell he is nervous.

He drops the box with MacDougall, who manages to seize the moment and flutter out into the living room.

"Still with the magic tricks?" Gramma asks, but it is not a question.

Leon yanks a light cord, bringing a terrible brightness to the scene.

There she is—just as I remember her—her wrinkles carved in disapproval, the gray eyebrows knit to a permanent frown.

My view returns, as usual, to Gramma's feet, which have escaped from the black heavy shoes and look surprisingly smaller, and sad, gnarled in peach stockings, with a corn pad, noticeable even through the cotton. Gramma without her shoes looks like the wicked witch after the water-pail dousing—she is shrunken and small in her old chair.

"I knew I should not have come," she greets us officially, "but something told me there was trouble up here. At Mimi's."

She beckons to me, her fingers curled like the claws on the chair. She opens her hand and I see it—the broken figurine, the headless boy.

"Very nice. My valuables—what else is broken?" she croaks. Then she stares at my face and adds: "Very nice, such makeup on a child."

"I'm twelve," I tell her, "and it was for a show."

"I won't say what it looks like."

She breathes heavily, exhaling a bitter scent into the room.

"So?" she repeats. "I see you ate all the chocolates, too. What is going on in here? Where is Mimi? Why is all this . . . allowed to happen? It's a . . . disgrace!"

"So!" Leon defies her. Then his voice softens. "Mimi asked me to stay with Zoya. She's in the hospital—"

"I knew it," Gramma says, but I can tell by the way the color leaves her face, turning her from a jaundiced yellow to white, that she did not know.

"So," she says, "it happens again. First my daughter Shirley, now Mimi."

Shirley. The name of the lost daughter, my mother's sister. The missing. The one whose death was so painful, it left Gramma draped in black, along with all her furnishings. Shirley, who took leave of this apartment long ago and left it a place without light or laughter.

"There's nothing new," Gramma says. "God has no imagination."

She is depressing, I think, but she has style.

"History repeats. Misery repeats. Shirley had no luck, and now . . . this."

"Gramma," I say, "everything will be all right."

But even as I say that, a memory returns—not my first memory, but some dark later memory. The name *Shirley* . . . I have heard Gramma say that name before. She walked the floor, repeating it over and over again . . . "Shirley, Shirley, Shirley . . . " That must have been when my mother's sister died, Gramma's older daughter. I could feel rather than see her grief, the sounds of croaking, rasping sobs and the smell of funeral flowers.

"Nothing is ever right, not for us." Gramma cannot stay sad; she prefers to be angry.

Leon goes to the kitchen. "Hey," he says, "how about some tea and cake?"

"You bake," she says with a disapproving tone.

"I bake!" he shoots back. "I bake big-time."

"I'm not surprised," she says.

She continues to amaze—how does she manage this? No matter what she says—the most innocent word becomes an insult, an indictment.

She occupies the corner of the living room like a shadow.

"When will you know?" she says. "About Mimi?"

There is an awful pause as Leon fumbles with plates and saucers and the teapot in the kitchen. And I am hearing his answer correctly: "We don't know."

Gramma has brought grief and darkness back into the house. She has also brought a new box of candy.

She offers it to me. Inside are chocolate-covered jelly shapes in the form of tropical animals. I remember the ritual from the past—I accept the candy and place one in my mouth. She watches me as I work the candy with my tongue, hoping it will melt and go down fast. This is the price she exacts for the candy—that she watches. As always, it takes away most, if not all, of my enjoyment.

"Thank you, Gramma," I say.

"You're very welcome. Try the little alligator."

I am eating a small chocolate-covered gummy pelican. I force myself to take the alligator and eat that too.

"I used to like those. Now I am not allowed," she says. "Have another."

Torture by candy, I think, as I sit there and eat one tropical chocolate animal after another. She surprises me, though, by producing a gift bag from beside the monster chair. "Here," she says, handing it to me. "It's a seashell. If you cup it to your ear, you can hear the sea."

I hold it and listen—there is a distant, remembered roar of waves and crashing surf. I can't help but smile—what a miracle!

"I can't hear anything anymore," Gramma says.

She wants to go to bed—her own bed—so Leon moves out of what had been Gramma's original bedroom and sits beside me on the sofa. We listen to Gramma moan and groan as she adjusts herself for what she insists will not be sleep. "I don't sleep, I lie there and rest. My legs hurt too much to let me sleep."

I feel sorry for Gramma, but scared—will her return cancel out my mother's?

We are both surprised when, in the morning, Gramma appears, drinks a cup of Leon's strong coffee, samples his cake, and gives me a kiss on the cheek.

"I love you," she says. "I love you," she repeats, kissing my cheek. "What's your name, child?"

"The worry is no good for me," Gramma says at the breakfast table. "What good am I here?"

We don't answer.

No good, I am thinking.

I am gluing the head on the china boy.

"You can't fix that—it was priceless," Gramma says.

Leon opens his palm: He holds an identical porcelain boy, with a head attached.

"More like $19.95," Leon remarks.

I look at him in wonder—when did he buy the replacement?

Not that it pleases Gramma.

"It's not the same quality. The one I had was more valuable. You cannot replace what is lost."

To my horror and Leon's shock, Gramma snaps the head off the new figurine.

"You see—how cheap!"

Maybe she is right. I wonder. Does tragedy repeat?

CHAPTER TEN

Pandora's Box

May 29, midnight

I am afraid to go to sleep. I have what I call "the bad feeling." I just lie there, listening to my heartbeat.

How strange it is, having Gramma back in the apartment, sleeping there in my mother's bedroom. She groans in her sleep. Leon is in the living room, where I am aware of his long form draped over the sofa, legs hanging off the arm.

I am afraid to go to the kitchen for a drink. It seems as if the apartment has been reclaimed, and it all belongs to Gramma.

And now it is happening again, that strange

night walk, the dream journey—I am floating, it seems, from 2B to a more distant place, a place where the moon shines not on flowering trees and the city, or even Roxy's Mansion, but upon a square cement prison sort of place, encrusted in ice. . . . I am walking, walking in circles, I cannot stop . . . I have no control. I see the snow fly, even though I know it's almost June . . . the flakes fall cold upon my face. . . . My mind is white, blank. I am frozen but I can feel a hand is upon my elbow, turning me around and back inside the building. Who is my savior? I turn and see Eugene, in his pajamas and a robe, the Disgusting Boy, guiding me back inside, up the stairs, to the door of 2B!

The door swings inward and there is Leon, eyes open wide in alarm.

The Disgusting Boy whispers, "I found her in the courtyard," and disappears. Was it really him?

Leon turns pale and his mouth is set. I don't know when he and Gramma decide that her visit is over, but when I come out of the bathroom in the early morning, Leon is holding out her umbrella. He bends then, like a knight in a fairy tale—but before the crone, not the princess Cinderella. Slowly, gently, he relaces her black shoes.

Leon escorts Gramma to the waiting taxi. I see them talking out in the courtyard, and I wonder what they are saying, planning. Will Gramma see my mother? Or is it, as she has said, "Too much to go through all over again"?

I watch the taxi pull away.

I keep the bathroom light lit, and Playful is in there sleeping, in the box we prepared in the tub, with my mother's soft chenille bathrobe, the special one with the roses, as her bedding. Playful whimpers again, and I keep trying to comfort her.

She is a nice little cat, and now when I rub her under the chin, she rolls over, and I can see she has a white star on her belly. She has licked herself much cleaner, and actually she is a very pale gray, not dark as I first thought.

Her belly is unbelievably big, and active. It moves as if a dozen kittens are kicking around inside her. She feels tight as a drum.

I am eager for her to have the kittens, but hope she waits till my mother returns. I worry, too, that something may go wrong—Playful might die giving birth, or her kittens might not survive.

I focus on the secrets—the locked-away letters, the suitcase. There must be an answer inside them somewhere. Am I ready to open the suitcase? Ready to know?

I hesitate, remembering the myth we read at school—Pandora's box. Did Pandora wish she had never opened the box?

As I open the suitcase, I gasp. The documents have shifted, and on top is a picture of a girl who looks like me but is maybe six years older. She is standing before a church with a gold, onion-shaped dome, and she wears dark socks that sag in wrinkles, a baggy coat, and a kerchief.

A teenage boy is standing with her—he is not posing but seems blurred, as if he is trying to step out of the frame. The date is the year before my birth.

I feel a shiver of recognition. I do not have to understand the words written in a thick black scrawled foreign alphabet—these are the Russian "birth parents," the ones I envision standing side by side when I was born, although of course she—the girl—would have had to be lying down on a hospital bed.

I see the documents have translations stapled to them. The names are unfamiliar, but I can recognize the purpose of this top page—it is the statement that they give up their right to the child described on the parchment. And of course, as my hand trembles, I know the child is me.

I recall the anger in my mother's voice when strangers would ask, "*Do you have any children of your own?*" "*Is she your real daughter?*" This girl, the birth mother, has deep-set eyes like mine; she is even wearing glasses. The boy is dark-haired like me; the girl is fair. Somehow, seeing them makes me miss my mother more. I want her here to explain, to tell me everything.

I think of searching for this girl and boy, but I feel my heart harden like a stone in my chest.

My throat is sore. I can't stop staring at my old clothes—the red kerchief and the black-and-white-checked dress—the clothes I was wearing when my mother found me. I pick up the dress. It is so tiny, worn, repaired by hand in a few places. By whose hand? Next, I see my shoes are here too—little black lace-up shoes, so worn, there are no heels left, and there is a hole in the sole.

I poke my finger through the hole, and a rush of sensation shoots through me, opening up the world of my childhood. I remember walking, feeling the cold through this shoe. I was standing there, alone and cold, and she picked me up—my mother. Mimi. She made me warm; she held me, and I know that forever, she is the only person who can ever save me. All the warmth of the world is between us, and she presses the pain from me when she hugs me good night.

She must come back now; I must not sleep. I must never go to sleep again until my mother comes home. Something terrible will happen if I relax my guard. The Buka is certainly here, and as soon as I surrender to sleep, sure enough, she will get me.

Yet as I close the suitcase, a spell seems to overcome me; a heavy sensation that is similar I think to being drugged or drinking a sleeping potion. I cannot resist. I am like Dorothy in the field of poppies. Now I fall down, down, down, and something awful will surely happen. I know another secret now—that dreams come true, especially bad ones. Dreams are an exit from our lives as we know them, a descent to hell. If we are really lucky, someone may pull us back, and hold us and keep the darkness away just a little while longer.

I have crossed through a black tunnel, the underworld of the Buka; Gramma is banished and dare I think that Leon has saved me? Have I returned to the light?

CHAPTER ELEVEN

The Buka

May 29, morning

I am queasy at breakfast.

We are having a pommelo, a kind of giant grapefruit, when a letter arrives for me. In my excitement, I half rip the envelope. My mother's message is nice, but her handwriting is strange. It is faint and wavy, as if sliding off the page. "I love you and I will be home on your birthday. A kiss to you and Natalie. Show Leon how we do things and don't be too hard on him!"

I check the postmark. She is in the city. I do not recognize the zip code, though.

I memorize the address.

"If I write to my mother, will you mail the letter?" I ask.

"Of course," Leon says.

I want to tell her about Playful and being Sonambula.

I write and write, three whole pages on my special stationery, and Leon takes my letter and says he will send it express mail, to be sure my mother receives it fast.

May 30, midnight

It's midnight. My birthday. My mother will be home today, but I can no longer wait. While Leon sleeps, I take all my savings, the fifteen dollars and fifty cents left from lunch, and creep from 2B. I have an address now. I know where she is, and I will find her.

Outside, gray drizzle falls. The Stone Girl looks damp and sad. No one is awake yet. At the nearest corner, where the buses go, I stand and watch for the next bus.

In the bus shelter, it smells of old pee and garbage. I am afraid to stand there, so I start walking. I can count the streets. It is maybe a hundred blocks to where my mother is hidden. I count them off and bend my head into the increasing rain.

After an hour, I am still eighty blocks away. I shiver and march through the chill. My feet hurt. My left foot, especially, has a blister. I march on, block after dreary block. The cars and trucks splash, as they speed by like boats through the flooding avenues.

The neighborhood is not so nice here. Garbage flies in the wind through wasted streets and alleys; a rat, humpbacked, crosses my path; a chained dog leaps and snarls from a doorway. This place seems like another country, far from the cozy yellow kitchen of home, far from my pink-purple-green bedroom.

I have a stitch in my side. I have to go to the bathroom, but I don't see a place to go, so I keep walking, walking. . . . I will not stop, I must not stop.

I am counting streets. I must reach 161st Street, where my mother is, where the hospital is. . . . I feel as if I am in my first shoes, the ones with the hole in the sole. My red sequin shoes are damp and dirtied; I splash through puddles at each curb. But I don't care how wet, how tired I am, I just keep walking, walking. . . . I will be there soon. . . .

It is morning and the day begins. People appear in work clothes. I feel I stand out with my purple glasses and dirty red sequin shoes. I am losing sequins, like drops of blood.

Finally, I am at the street. I look up and see the sign—161st Street. But there is nothing here: a vacant street and a car-repair lot. A man lies in the gutter, not moving while the rain beats down on him.

A big woman in a black cape raincoat swoops over to me, and I know who she is before she speaks. "What are you doing here?" she says, yelling into the rain.

I name the hospital where my mother is staying.

"You are on the wrong side of town," she

says. "You aren't anywhere near there."

She points, and I see the river, moving like rainbow-tinted sludge, slick with oil.

"That hospital is on the other side of the city, near the river."

I follow her pointing finger, and see how hopeless it is—I cannot get to what seems to be a grim fortress so very far away. I sway, feeling my knees weaken, and I see gold dots in the rain-filled air. I know this feeling from long ago, from the beginnings of everything that was bad—I am cold and wet and alone, and I have no mother anymore.

It is almost a relief to surrender, to swoon and fall to the pavement, and know her black cape will swallow me up and I, too, will disappear. The Buka has won.

In the darkness that is the Buka, I see myself in the checked dress, the red kerchief, and the shoes with the holes.

That young girl in the photo, my first mother, is leading me into the low brown building, the orphanage. It is winter, and ice hangs like daggers from every gutter and drain. I don't want to go in—I want to go home. She is crying but saying, in another language, words I can understand—she doesn't want to leave me, but she can no longer take care of me. *Please,* I beg her. *Don't leave me here.* It doesn't matter if we are cold; it doesn't matter if we have no food. Just hold me close.

That first mother—I can remember now—we shared a big bed, pressed against the wall. I can recall the sound of her voice in that other language; I cry my name for her: Mamotchka, Mamotchka, Mamotchka. She whispered bedtime stories then, but even the stories seemed sad. She told the same story again and again—the little Snow Girl.

Yes, I think of the whole story again, and now I remember the end—an old couple who could not have a baby made a beautiful girl out of snow. The girl lived on ice porridge, just like the slush I drank in my frozen bottles. She had to stay outside or melt, and one day she wandered off into the forest. Several animals—a bear, a wolf—offered to lead her home. But the snow girl trusted only one—a fox. The fox kept his word and returned her to the old couple, her "parents," and he asked for a plump hen as a reward. But the parents thought, "We have our snow girl back; why lose the hen?" So they tricked the fox and put a fierce dog in a bag, and the dog leaped out and attacked the fox, who fled . . . but so did the snow girl, for she felt her parents did not love her more than they valued a hen. She went back forever to the white land of ice—to frost and snow, where she belonged because her parents did not love her enough.

"Wipe your feet, Zoya," the first mother is saying. "Scrape the ice from your shoes before you go inside." There is a railing; I grab the railing, and I will not let go. I will never let go. My hands freeze onto the metal. My first mother is tugging me, crying and pleading—"Let go, let go! You must go inside!"

I hang on to the rail. Never! I will never go in there. I want to go home with my mother, even if it is only to starve, lying on a ragged bed by a dirt-streaked frozen window.

My first mother is crying; it is so cold, her tears freeze into icicles. I beg her to pick me up, to take me home. She seems to give in; wearily she says, "All right, Zoya, just let go." I release my fingers from the rail. At that moment, she yells for help, and the big one, a monstrously tall woman from inside—the Buka—comes out on the steps of the orphanage. Betraying me, my first mother says, "You take her. I can't anymore."

And so the Buka descends upon me with her big black cloak, and she tackles me and drags me kicking and screaming into the prison.

I am the snow girl, turned back into snow. Later, trapped in the barred crib, I taste the ice in my bottle. My parents did not love me enough. I have no one. I might as well die.

"I'm here," someone is saying, "I'm here." But who can save me now? Two arms are lifting me up as if I really were a baby.

I open my eyes and stare into the blue eyes of The Astounding Armand. Leon.

He scoops me up into a warm hug. There is

a taxicab. He carries me to the cab and rests me gently on the backseat. He holds me, saying over and over again that I am not alone, that he is there with me, and my mother will soon come home. My shivers have nothing to do with the cold. Fear mixed with relief has taken over my body and is moving it like some coiled metal toy. Will I ever stop shaking?

CHAPTER TWELVE

Birthday

May 30, 5 P.M.

I slept in all morning. Leon woke me in the afternoon and wished me a happy birthday. My mother is still not home. The world looks different to me now, as if the moon shines by day. In the courtyard, the Stone Girl stands pelted by heavy, sheeting rain. She waits for the magic moment when she will come back to life. Meanwhile, she stands in her permanent pool of old black leaves. The circular base of the fountain pedestal cracked long ago, and the water drains, leaving behind the matted leaves.

Leon says, "Let's buy a cake and decorate it,"

but I say, "No. That's what I do with my mother; I can wait."

His face falls, but I know many secret charms, and I know if I do things with him that I always did with my mother, it is quite possible she will never return. If I hold out, it is as if I have saved her place. Flynn has always agreed—"Do not change anything. Your mother will come home. Everything will be as it was."

I rip a page from my diary and stuff it in my place of safekeeping—the inner hollow cone of Natalie with the tiny key. As I place the rolled scrap of paper in there, I feel what Flynn's mom, Mrs. Sheila, calls a psychic shiver. I fall onto my bed as if onto a landing strip.

I feel myself curl into a ball, and I start to claw my sheets. I can't stop, and I know that I have done this before . . . long ago. My feet are kicking and I am screaming. I am back in Russia and the Buka is back for real. I know her now; she caught me when I was four years old and dragged me past the frozen gate. I kicked and screamed, but no one came to save me, no one loved me, no one cared.

Leon is sitting on the edge of my bed, holding my hand; his face gray with exhaustion. "I love her too, you know," he says.

I do know, but it doesn't help.

Why did I sense this bad ending all along?

I take my diary and begin to rip more pages.

"Stop," Leon begs. "She wants you to keep it. Don't destroy your diary."

My mother gave the diary to me, but she will never see it. Whatever has happened, she has gone. I rip another page, crumple it.

"Okay. Go ahead," Leon says, to my surprise. "Let it out. Rip it, and scream all you want." He shakes his head sadly. "I didn't see this coming."

He looks odd. His doves have fluttered over to him and perch on his shoulders.

I know he is trying to help, but nobody can help me now. She has not come, and I think she never will. She has never been this late before.

He says something Mimi once told me: "Sometimes, even when they want to, parents cannot keep a promise." Does Leon think she's not coming home too?

I rock to and fro, bite my pillow. There is violence in my blood, and I know how close anger is to grief. I cry and cry, until, somehow, I descend, in those terrible yanking stages, down to some deep pit of blackness.

Leon holds me and we both cry, until we can cry no longer, and then we lie there, emptied of our tears, still in our grief. I listen—there is no such thing as complete silence—as the refrigerator hums in the kitchen. There is a distant clank of the elevator cables and beeps and buzzes from other apartments.

From far off, even through thick walls, I can detect the voices of other families calling out to one another. I hear other children shout "Mom" or "Mother." Not in need but in their usual routine—out there, beyond my cell of loneliness, are children at home with their parents, and their cries are for ordinary causes—they want something to eat, ice cream, or money for the movies.

Leon hands me another letter from my mother, but now I am too scared to open it. The postmark is the same as the first. The letters were mailed together. I know before reading it what my mother will have written—that she loves me and will be home soon, but it is too late.

Now I know that her letters are lies, false messages sent to make me feel safe.

"Don't worry," Leon repeats, "everything will be all right. I promise."

My mother promised too, I thought, and she always kept her promises. Until today. If she is not home now, she must be . . . I cannot finish my thought.

"Your mother will come home," Leon says. He reaches over and holds me tight. "I swear to you, your mother will come home!"

Leon lies on the floor in my room like a faithful dog. Is he afraid that I will sleepwalk again? Run away? Or perhaps, like the snow girl, return to the land of frost?

I hear a moan from my bathroom. I investigate—Playful is lying on her side, looking up at me, her front paws crossed. She lies on my mother's robe in the tub. Her big belly seems to work on its own. Waves pass through the fur, and as I watch, a glistening bag protrudes under her tail, and plop, a little package drops to the floor of the tub, shining as if in plastic wrap.

I watch, hypnotized, as Playful licks the sack, and the tiniest kitten, miniature ears flat, eyes shut, fur short and sticking up, appears. There is bright-pink blood on the beautiful bathrobe of my mother's that I gave her as a nest . . . but I dare not move the robe.

Playful has a look, like the Stone Girl, of ancient recognition. Her eyes do not leave mine. The second gleaming bundle pokes forth and Playful repeats the process. The first kitten is round bellied, toddling on its four paws to snuggle against her belly. Playful's bubblegum-pink nipples poke forth, offering the first treat. Within minutes, more kittens squeeze out and she licks them clean.

Five baby kittens emerge, and all fasten on to nurse. The bathtub and the circled cushion of the chenille bathrobe become a mass of vibrating, purring little furred bodies. Then, just when I thought the last kitten was born, another slippery package plops onto the robe, but this time

Playful looks up at me, exhausted. I watched her clean all the others, so I take a little facecloth and rub the sixth kitten till the covering, like see-through plastic, slips off, and this last baby begins to breathe and purr and seek out her warm mother's milk.

Playful looks up at me in what I interpret as cat gratitude. She nips the little rope that ties her to the last kitten, and this baby too becomes separate and alive and wriggling beside her.

I get up and call for Leon to come see.

He runs to the bathroom and stands, stunned, above the tub. "You didn't see this coming, did you, Leon?" I tease.

"I never saw anything like this," he admits, smiling.

I kneel beside the bathtub filled with baby kittens and the proud mother, who lies, eyes shut, in a deep purr.

Later that night Mrs. Sheila comes up to 2B with a frozen strudel and sets a candle on it and says, "Make a wish." She serves the strudel with cherry soda. Everything she likes is sweet and pink.

"It don't matter what you eat or don't eat," confides Mrs. Sheila. "It's all written in the big book. If your number's up and it's your time, you go."

"Go where?" I ask, confused.

"Down there," she answers.

I guess she means hell, but I picture Mr. Uzzle's basement.

"You know," she says, adding some whiskey to her cherry soda, "I can see the future, honey, and you got a lot to look forward to, if you don't fall down and give up."

When I refuse to blow out my candle and make a wish, Leon says, "*I* have a wish, Zoya, and you can make it come true."

He wants to do one more magic show, to prove we can do it. "Please," he says.

"Oh, do it!" Mrs. Sheila says. "I never saw the show! And you know I can see the future, and I can tell you—this is something you should do! Show everyone Sonambula! You can do it!"

I have a wish too—to consult the Stone Girl.

We go outside where she stands radiant, ready to dance. As we gaze at her, I become aware of another presence in the courtyard. I turn around and see the Disgusting Boy, Eugene.

He watches us with such misery on his crusted face. Suddenly I realize maybe he is not so disgusting after all? He led me home that one time I sleepwalked; maybe he watches us to help, not to spy? I look at Leon and nod toward the Disgusting Boy.

Together we go over to Eugene, and I say, "Look, Eugene. I do strange things sometimes, because"—I bite my lip—"my mother is gone."

"Mine, too," he says simply. "I'm sorry."

"I know you're sorry," I tell him.

A look passes between us.

Leon offers to show Eugene some magic tricks. I look at Leon, who has never spoken of his own parents, and suddenly, I know without being told that someone left Leon too, long ago. Now he makes people and objects disappear—and reappear. Leon looks at Eugene. "Want to help with the magic act?" he asks.

"Can I play with the doves?" Eugene asks.

"If you handle them gently."

Flynn, Eugene, and I practice with Leon all the next day.

At dusk, we walk a few blocks to a corner nightclub called, simply, Roxy's, where green neon bulbs blink on and off.

"They never did magic here before, but there is always a first time," says Leon. "The show will be here, tonight!" I wish my mother were here to see me perform.

May 31, 8 P.M.

I will give this journal to my mother whenever she returns. I must have faith.

"The show must go on," Leon says, and I now know he means I must be as strong as my mother is, even though it is so hard to wait.

"Your mother would want you to do it," he says. "Remember, she was the first Sonambula."

And so Leon and I, Flynn, the Disgusting Boy (whom I will from now on always call

Eugene), and Mrs. Sheila all walk to Roxy's, where a sign has been posted—THE ASTOUNDING ARMAND AND SONAMBULA!

This time, despite my inner ache, the rawness in my throat, and the hollow in my belly, I do not miss my beat. When it is time, I swing into position, and I release the birds on cue. Leon dances with me, and then with the Dancing Cane. I feel an odd joy, as if I have left myself behind. I hear the music and feel the heat of the stage lights. I release Nicky, and the cockatiel flies onto Leon's head, to a huge burst of applause.

"And now, for the first time ever," Leon announces, "we will show you a new illusion—the Levitating Girl!"

I lie down on the table. Leon moves to center stage. "If this works," I whisper, "everything and anything is possible."

"Concentrate," he answers. "I can do some of the magic, but not all."

I concentrate on happy outcomes—for my mother, for myself, for Leon, even for Eugene. And I feel it, I really do, the mysterious force that will make me rise. I felt something this magical only once before—when I saw the northern lights in my own living room and knew, for an instant, the Secret of Life. The enemy of that light is the Buka. But now I know I must attract the light myself. Without my mother, without Leon, I must defeat fear and the darkness that escorts the Buka. It is up to me. My mother says: "If you believe in her, she will win." I must not let her win. Someday, my mother will die and leave me, but I will continue to love her for as long as I live, and so will Leon. And maybe that is the Secret of Life—that love is something bigger and finer than the shadow witch!

And now I know another secret, and am sworn not to tell how: I can levitate! Leon raises his large white hand over me, the music plays, and I feel myself rise. My body leaves the table-top, and I hover in midair.

"Trust yourself!" Leon whispers.

I trust with all my might, and float in a radiant bubble. The music reaches a crescendo, and I give myself completely to the light and air—I do not fall, because Leon is there to catch me. I feel what I have known only in dreams, or when I walked in my sleep—I do, I do have the ability to fly! If I believe I can, my mind can soar, my hopes can raise me into the air . . . this is not a trick! I am reborn. My life flashes backward through the darkness of the Buka and Gramma and into this radiant dazzle. I will win!

Mrs. Sheila and Flynn clap the loudest. Then we all walk home to Roxy's Mansion in the late-night silence. The air is still moist, but warming. "Wow," says Eugene, who we now notice has a fresh-scrubbed face and a clean windbreaker. "Could you do that at our school?"

"How about for the dance!" says Flynn. "How cool would that be?"

The dance. I think of my dress hanging in my closet. Dances are not for me. I am not one of the popular girls; I am Zoya, the strange one. . . .

But now I am Sonambula; I am Zoya, who can fly, levitate, and conquer the Buka.

"Yes," I say to Flynn. "Let's go!"

The next night, we march en force—Eugene, Flynn, Leon, and I—to the school gym.

The decorations are hanging and the ginger ale is flowing. A giant bowl of pink punch sits ready. There are massive bowls of potato chips.

The mood in the gym is not festive. The boys all stand on one side and the girls on the other, as if they were there to play basketball. The music teacher, Mrs. Frobish, a thin redhead, is waving her white arms and saying, "Hey, let's dance!" But no one is moving.

As if on cue, Eugene starts to walk to the boys' side of the gym.

Flynn and I huddle, pretending we are talking to each other so we don't look weird. Song after song plays, but no one wants to be first to go onto the polished dance floor.

Mrs. Frobish, in desperation, begins to sing! She has a weak voice, on key, but she looks strange singing a teenage rock song about longing for a boyfriend.

I give Leon our secret sign. He nods and darts out the door. He returns wheeling his shining black trunk and wearing his top hat and cape. Then he steps to the center of the stage and accepts the mike from the exhausted Mrs. Frobish.

Eugene, losing his shyness, steps forward and addresses the crowd. "The Astounding Armand . . . and Sonambula!" he announces.

We do a stripped-down version of our routine, but I know the showstopper will be the Dancing Cane. The lights are lowered and a rainbow spot hits Leon just right. The white-tipped cane rises into midair—levitating as I did—and floats across the gym. I have seen Leon dance with the cane before, but never with such agility and grace. He manages to reach both sides of the gym, to weave among the girls and boys. The music plays on, and he delivers a magnificent finale. . . . I produce the feather flower bouquet and take my own short bow.

As we hoped, the Dancing Cane worked like a magic wand over the crowd. The girls begin to dance first, singly and then in pairs. Soon Eugene gets up his nerve and asks me to dance. I step forward and look at his chest, rather than into his eyes. We are the first boy-girl combination on the floor.

Now everyone will say we are going out. That is not true. It is better that we are just friends; it doesn't matter what they think. Out of the corner of my eye, I see Flynn march across the gym and ask the best-looking boy in the class to dance. The next thing I know, they are flying around the room!

Now all kinds of combinations are formed, and the beat picks up. We are dancing faster and faster, and the lights are flowing, rainbow hued, too, as if now all of us have entered those northern lights I knew so long ago. The disco ball glitters like Mrs. Sheila's crystal ball. All is sparkle; how my mother would adore it: girls in sheer dresses, hair flying; the boys catching us as we spin. I could dance like this forever. And in that rainbow spinning, for the first time I feel free.

Later, exhausted but exhilarated, we walk the steep block back up to Roxy's Mansion. The stars are out; even the city lights cannot dim the Big Dipper tonight.

When we reach the courtyard, I see the Stone Girl. In a flash, I clearly remember walking dreamily up to her after midnight, thinking she was cold and covering her with my Mickey.

And now like the Stone Girl, I, too, have spent the night dancing.

When I wake up the next morning, fine rain is silvering the courtyard.

Suddenly Nicky squawks a series of high, excited cries.

I crane my neck and see, small as a bumblebee in the distance, a yellow cab approach our building. I hold my breath and pray.

And then I see her in her wraparound coat, holding it closed against the drizzle. She walks, taking small steps, past the dogwood tree and the Stone Girl. I see another woman holds her arm—to my shock, it is Mrs. Sheila!

I rise and run, still in my nightgown, and call for Leon to follow. "She's here!" I call. "She's come home! She's home!"

I run so hard, I stumble on the stairs. Nothing matters now, nothing but that I reach my mother, touch her, and feel that she is real. I run through the mist and rain—she is standing there, with an overnight bag at her feet. Leon reaches her first and grabs the bag. "Let me take that, Mimi." Mrs. Sheila gives me her "psychic" look and darts inside her storefront. "You'll need some privacy," she predicts as she leaves.

My mother leans for a moment as if she could faint.

"Oh, Zoya," she says, reaching out for me. "I'm so sorry I'm late! I missed your birthday!"

I am crying for joy so hard, I can't even tell her it doesn't matter; nothing matters except that she came back. I notice now that she is moving a little stiffly, and she holds herself so that her left side is turned slightly away, against the pressure of my hug. Leon holds the overnight bag and has a firm grip on her elbow, as if he is afraid she will fall. I feel my mother's cheek, so fresh and cold against mine, and she whispers, "Hurry, you're not even dressed—let's get inside."

Inside 2B, the apartment is a glorious mess, and we collapse upon one another in hugs and kisses.

"I'm sorry," she says. "I should have told you more, but I was scared, and I thought you would be frightened if you knew more. . . ."

I lean against my mother's chest, so happy to have her home.

"Careful," my mother whispers. "I'd better tell you now. I had to go. I had . . . I had . . . an operation." Her voice breaks. "The exploratory—it was serious and it had to be done right away. . . . I am going to look like your old doll, Natalie." She gives a twisted smile.

She looks up at Leon. "I am so grateful Leon offered to come here and stay."

Leon smiles, shrugs. "I was glad to be of service."

"He slept by the end of my bed," I report.

My mother's eyes meet Leon's, and I feel a beam flash between them. " 'Thank you' doesn't say it," my mother says to Leon.

"You don't have to thank me," Leon says.

"Now you're all better and you will never leave me again?" I say to my mother.

She pauses, and we sit together, rocking on the couch. I am trying to get onto her lap without pressing against the tender spot.

"I think I have to tell you a secret now," my mother says. "Sometimes we don't have definite answers. . . . I think I will be all right. But no one really knows . . . we don't know very much at all. . . . You know I had the sickness that killed my sister?"

"Shirley," I whisper.

"Medicine is better now," my mother says, "but the truth is no one can be sure. You know I had—" Her voice catches on the ugly barbed word, the clawed word, "cancer." I see it as a crab that began to devour her but was caught and stopped.

"I think I will be all right, and maybe I should have told you more . . . but I didn't know much myself until the operation. They explored and found it. It's a hard thing, because of my sister."

Her words catch me short. I see she is speaking the truth, a truth she fears I cannot accept. This is my turn to show her I understand more than she thinks.

"I know some secrets too," I offer. "I know sometimes you love someone and cannot stay. . . ."

Leon repacks his doves in their travel boxes

and prepares to leave as quietly as he arrived. He is averting his gaze as he picks up his music sheets, books, top hats, and canes. I see him looking for the odd loose end; then he puts his set of keys on the entry bench. That shocks me—his surrender of the keys. He won't be living here anymore. Is it his turn to disappear now?

We watch him pack the trunk and the silken scarves. I relax against my mother's good side and feel her arm around my shoulder. Leon walks over to us; he is carrying the case the doves use for travel and is tugging his trunk on its rolling wheels. I can hear the doves coo deep within their boxes.

He offers me a gift-wrapped package, and I open it and see my costume, but with a badge embroidered on it, my award for a "stellar performance as Sonambula." He gives me a scroll, too, that has my "Official Membership" in the Society of Magicians.

"What exactly went on while I was away?" my mother asks; her eyes have their old twinkle, and I can see that she is almost laughing again.

"Zoya starred as my assistant," Leon tells her. "She was just as talented as her mother."

"Leon," I say, going to him before he can disappear, "I want my mother to see our show. You can't really leave, not right now!"

And so we perform again—The Astounding Armand and Sonambula. I run to my room and put on my costume—the glittery leotard, tights, and feather boas and my sparkling red sequin shoes. Leon dons his collapsible top hat and the sweeping black-satin, red-lined magician's cape.

Leon plays the music on his boom box—"A Summer Place." We stand in the center of the living room, while my mother sits watching on the sofa. The doves appear and disappear, and this time both Leon and I dance with the magic cane.

As the wings flutter, my mother claps. "I would never have believed you could learn so much magic so fast!"

"I have the best teachers," I say, looking at them both.

Again, that odd flash between them—why

do they like each other so much, yet always go their separate ways?

"Where are you going now?" I ask Leon.

"I am returning to my old address—'Whereabouts Unknown.'"

"But you will write to me?"

"Of course, and I will send you gifts from all over the world."

"You don't have to spend a lot of money," I say. "A card or a letter is good, with maybe a ruby or two thrown in . . ."

"Or a pearl . . ." Then he adds, with his funny, uneven smile, "I want you to know, Zoya, if you ever want me to appear, you can call this top secret classified number, and it will find me wherever I am, even if I am on the other side of the world, and I will reappear here in 2B before you can say 'The Astounding Armand.'"

"Really?" I accept a small card, which has the design of a top hat and his Dancing Cane—but the man on the card is invisible.

"Now you see me, now you don't!" he says.

"This is certainly true," my mother says, and her eyes crinkle, but her mouth doesn't smile—I wonder if once, long ago, she wanted Leon to stay and never again disappear.

He doesn't remove his cape and hat.

"I'm off," he says, and then laughs. "I should tell you—there is a white dinner in the fridge, a birthday baked Alaska in the freezer, and a litter of newborn kittens in the bathtub," he says, his eyes meeting my mother's.

"I want to name a kitten for you," I tell him, rushing to hug him. "The Astounding . . . but for short we can call him Asto!"

I have had this in my mind, because my favorite of the kittens—the last born—has a magic white star on his forehead, and he has shown, already, a talent for disappearing—even in the bathtub. His little tail sticks straight up, and he cuddles under my mother's bathrobe. If his tail didn't stick up, I could never find him. "I want to keep Asto: I remember his birth; I helped him come into the light!"

"All right," my mother agrees. "We'll keep Asto so we always have an Astounding around the house."

Leon leaves, tugging his trunk, with the bird

boxes stacked on top. My mother and I listen to the final click of our door, the sound of the elevator. The draft of his departure seems to blow the curtain at the window.

My mother and I go to the window and look down—Leon is crossing the courtyard; we see the yellow taxi waiting to take him, but he stops and turns to stand beside the Stone Girl. As if he can feel our eyes upon him, Leon then turns around and looks straight up at us and tips his hat.

Leon and my mother exchange a look, and I know that they will always love each other. Leon looks at me for a long moment, then turns, and we see him disappear, for real, but not forever. The taxi pulls away, taking him, and the doves, to their unknown destination.

"Whereabouts unknown." I finger the business card in my hand. I will call him, some midnight, I think, and I do trust he will reappear.

Later, in my room, my mother helps me tape together the pages of this midnight diary. We sit close, cuddled on my bed, like in the old days, and together we read.

Was it only ten days? I am amazed at how much happened, how far I have traveled.

My mother kisses my forehead, and she has tears in her eyes. She promises she will always tell me the complete truth from now on, even if it frightens us both.

"You know Gramma was never the same after my sister died. . . . She was always scared I would die young too. I'm sorry, Zoya. I thought of you as a small child who could not stand to know. . . . You suffered so as a baby; I didn't want you to worry."

"Gramma was here," I tell her, "and something happened."

"I know," my mother says. "She came to the hospital, too. Please understand if you can't forgive her. She is seventy-eight, and her heart broke long ago, when she lost Shirley."

"She said she loved me," I say, "but then she could not remember my name."

"She calls me Shirley sometimes. Just remember the good part—that she was moved to say she loves you."

We look at each other without speaking, and

we do not even have to say our *love you*'s tonight. The magic of hearing each other's thoughts is the single mystery that remains: I can hear my mother think, and she can hear me too, and we both are thinking *I love you* as the clock strikes twelve.

ACKNOWLEDGMENTS

I wish to thank the following for their inspiration:

Alexandra Rose Cunningham, Jasmine Zoie Cunningham, Corah Lin Walker, Maya Shengold, and Chelsey Raponi. My deep appreciation to Laura Geringer and Jill Santopolo for their devoted efforts and attentiveness to this book while in progress.

And I must acknowledge the soulful if silent output of our furred and feathered friends—Nikki, Playful, Tallie, Dakota, Ginger, and Spike.